"What's Your First Question For Our Contestants, Honey?"

the game-show host asked.

"I'd love to know what each guy would want to do on our first date." She spaced her words slowly, deliciously apart, as she'd been instructed.

The audience cheered at contestants number one and two's answers. Then the cowboy, number three, cleared his throat and said, "Maybe a movie. Maybe dinner, after...." The slow, deep drawl intrigued her. The man was reluctant. If she *had* to spend a weekend with a strange man, she preferred a really reluctant one.

Her masquerade as a stunning blonde was like playing Cinderella. Her friends would never guess her indentity—who would know she was just plain Chastity from Charlie's Auto filing and bookkeeping department? Certainly not the cowboy....

Dear Reader,

Q. What does our heroine know about the hero when she first meets him?
A. Not much!

His personality, background, family—his entire life—is a total mystery. I started to think that the heroine never *truly* knows what's in store for her when she first sees the hero. In fact, *her* life from that moment on can be likened to an adventure with a "mysterious" man. And it's from these thoughts that our Valentine's Day promotion, MYSTERY MATES, was born. After all, who *is* this guy and what *is* he looking for?

Each of our heroes this month is a certain type of man, as I'm sure you can tell from the title of each February Desire book. The *Man of the Month* by Raye Morgan is *The Bachelor* . . . a man who never dreamed he'd have anything to do with—*children!* Cait London brings us *The Cowboy,* Ryanne Corey *The Stranger,* Beverly Barton *The Wanderer* and from Karen Leabo comes *The Cop.*

Peggy Moreland's hero, *The Rescuer,* is a very special man indeed. For while his story is completely fictitious, the photo on the cover is that of a Houston, Texas, fire fighter. Picked from a calendar the Houston Fire Department creates for charity, this man is truly a hero.

So, enjoy our MYSTERY MATES. They're sexy, they're handsome, they're lovable . . . and they're only from Silhouette Desire.

Lucia Macro
Senior Editor

CAIT
LONDON
THE COWBOY

SILHOUETTE *Desire*

Published by Silhouette Books New York

America's Publisher of Contemporary Romance

Thank you, Kerry. Happy Valentine's Day.

SILHOUETTE BOOKS
300 East 42nd St., New York, N.Y. 10017

THE COWBOY

Copyright © 1993 by Lois Kleinsasser

ISBN: 0-373-05763-6

First Silhouette Books printing February 1993

All the characters in this book have no existence outside the imagination of the author and have no relation whatsoever to anyone bearing the same name or names. They are not even distantly inspired by any individual known or unknown to the author, and all incidents are pure invention.

® and ™: Trademarks used with authorization. Trademarks indicated with ® are registered in the United States Patent and Trademark Office, the Canada Trade Mark Office and in other countries.

Printed in the U.S.A.

CAIT LONDON

lives in the Missouri Ozarks but grew up in Washington and still loves craggy mountains and the Pacific Coast. She's a full-time secretary, a history buff and an avid reader who knows her way around computers. She grew up painting landscapes and wildlife—but is now committed to writing and enjoying her three creative daughters. Cait has big plans for her future—learning to fish, taking short trips for research and meeting people. She also writes as Cait Logan and has won the *Romantic Times* Best New Romance Writer award for 1986.

A Letter from the Author

Dear Reader:

The summer of my eighteenth year, I took the Greyhound bus to Yellowstone Park and worked at the Old Faithful area. There, washing dirty dishes (he was the *chief* dishwasher) was Mr. Twenty-One, Tall, Dark, and Gorgeous. Our romance began amid the park's natural beauty, roaming bears and the typical tourist question: "When do you turn on the geysers?"

The Firehole River ran warm and bubbly that day, and life and love were wonderful. The thrill of the favorite swimming spot was to jump off a ledge of rocks into the sweeping stream and let it carry you to a wider, lazy spot. I jumped first, mistaking the distance to the deeper channel. Water and bubbles passed over my head, my leg scraped by the lava rock. Then someone tugged me to the surface and I clung to my guy. Amid sweet kisses and warm water, he soothed my fears. Again the day was dreamy.

We drifted along in the sun and our inner tubes, looking forward to our employee sack lunches. The bears enjoyed them on the bank while we watched from the Firehole River, safely wrapped in each other's arms.

I remember that summer as one long date, filled with square dances, moonlit nights, old movies, geysers and romance. When he put me on the homeward-bound bus, my heart ached with his last "I love you."

Sincerely,

Cait London

One

Lucas Walkington studied the reflection of the television studio's overhead lights in his polished Western boots. He shifted uncomfortably, preferring his rangeland to Chicago's maze of concrete buildings that encircled the studio. He was picturing his Oklahoma ranch lying cool and springtime-sweet in the pink glow of dawn, when the show's theme song suddenly began. The host of "Heartbeats" took center stage and the crowd applauded loudly, eagerly awaiting the sensual banter between the show's contestants.

Valentine's Day meant Lucas gave his girls presents and they cooked a special dinner for him; it didn't mean he acted like a yahoo, offering himself up on some baby doll's dinner plate for a handful of tiny gold hearts while an entire nation watched and hooted.

The studio chair lacked the comfort of his favorite saddle. His competitors leaned forward, listening intently to the "Heartbeats" host. After a warm-up joke, the host issued the audience's preshow instructions. Ginger, a previous contestant, was unable to return to the show. A new "Heartbeat Goddess" named Honey would take Ginger's slot. Honey was described as every man's dream girl—a delicious blond confection—and after asking questions of each male contestant, she would choose her male "Heartbeat" for a luxurious weekend near Las Vegas.

That male contestant would return, brag about his weekend romance to coast-to-coast viewers, and choose from three new female contestants; thus "Heartbeats" rolled on across America.

Lucas ground his back teeth together and glanced at the other men seated behind the curtain with him. Ten years younger than Lucas's thirty-eight, El Toro's and Dream Guy's expressions lighted with excitement. Wearing winter tans, gold chains and loose designer shirts and trousers, they leaned forward in their chairs. Lucas settled back, crossing his long legs at the ankle. He studied the crease in his jeans and decided to settle back while El Toro and Dream Guy took the lead in the sensual banter with Honey.

He'd waited out droughts and dry pocketbooks, his seventeen-year-old twin daughters' scrapes with life, and fate still wasn't satisfied. Slapped with the stage label of The Love Bandit, Lucas concentrated on his boots; if he had a lick of horse sense, he'd stand up and hightail it back to Oklahoma.

A young woman assistant, a few years older than his daughters, smiled invitingly at him, and Lucas scowled back. The show was saturated with sensual heat, onstage and off. All he needed was some underage baby doll sidling up to him.

Sweat trickled down the back of his neck into the collar of his shirt. The glaring lights added to the heat of his shirt and sweater. His daughters had picked out his red designer sweater—after they entered his name in Tulsa's Lonesome Cowboy contest. They had taunted, tormented and teased him into appearing on the television program. To prove to his daughters, Summer and Raven, that he wasn't entirely "out of it," untuned to the pains of living and loving—to prove he hadn't completely turned one-hundred-percent certified old hermit—Lucas had reluctantly submitted to being coached and groomed for the dateable bachelor contest.

The contest promoted Oklahoma tourism and offered a prize of five thousand dollars in return for appearing on the widely televised dating program in Chicago.

Elated when Lucas won the Tulsa competition, the twins were ecstatic when he was chosen as a delegate to "Heartbeats." For the moment, they were angelic, a situation that could revert in half a shake of a prairie dog's tail.

The beautiful, six-foot, lanky twins were destined for trouble from the moment of their conception. Alesha, their mother, decided at the twins' birth that she'd had enough of scrimping and hardships on Lucas's remote ranch, and had yanked them into Tulsa with her parents. Later, when they were three, Alesha did not want the responsibility of "taming the tomboys." When the twins prepared Lucas for his "Heartbeats" debut, he began to understand a little of Alesha's fear. His daughters had tugged the new sweater across his broad shoulders and rumpled his hair, their blue eyes widening. Summer had exclaimed, "Dad, you are really a st— You really look hot!"

Then Raven had added quietly, "Ah...for, ah...someone your age, that is."

His tanned fingers gripped his thighs, and Lucas traced the scar caused by barbed wire. The host—Lyle Drake—ran through El Toro's and Dream Guy's advertising backers. Lucas lowered his jaw into his open collar as Lyle—a man who wore buffed fingernails and shoe lifts—introduced the Love Bandit. The Bandit's skin warmed, and a drop of salty sweat burned in his new razor cut. Somewhere in Lyle's introduction lurked the words "a tall, tanned hunk of Oklahoma cowboy beef."

The "beef" wondered darkly how Lyle would look with his designer rear end squishing a fresh cow pile.

The host of "Heartbeats" listed the show's many sponsors and the prizes awaiting the contestants at the different levels of competition. The Bandit's Oklahoma sponsors received their advertising due, and Lucas concentrated on the amount of interest five thousand dollars in appearance money would draw in the twins' college fund.

Lucas took a deep breath, preparing to shed the inane sensual banter with as much grace as he could scavenge. He would sit back and let the other yahoos take the lead. El Toro and Guy were frothing at the mouth, ready to party.

With a bit of luck, Lucas would be eliminated early in the rounds of questioning. He'd be so dull, so dumb, that he'd be dropped quicker than a cornered skunk.... The Heartbeat Goddess would select a weekend player and he could slink back to his ranch to hole up until the whole mess was forgotten.

While waiting to be introduced on "Heartbeats," Chastity Beauchamp shot an angry glare at her half-sister, Hope.

Chastity inhaled sharply, uncomfortable in the tight, confining bra and low-cut, slinky dress Hope had chosen for her to wear. Black, off-the-shoulder, hugging every curve until the hem touched her thighs, the dress represented everything that Chastity was not—sexy, available and ready to play.

Chastity crushed Hope's prepared list of questions for the waiting dateables. Her sister had drafted the wrong person to fill a vacancy on the show's lineup. Chastity pressed her lips together, then parted them as she remembered her sister's instructions for glamour. Hope had applied gloss and color for "wet, dewy lucious lips."

Adjusting her tightly closed fingers to avoid damaging a false nail that Hope had carefully applied, Chastity duly licked her lips as she had been instructed. In her lifetime role as family supporter, she had played many roles for many disasters, each worse than the last. Hope's latest disaster had laid a guilt trip right at Chastity's practical shoes.

Chastity wished for those comfortable shoes now, rather than the stiletto heels that made her legs appear longer.

"If you don't take the empty slot on the Valentine's Day show, Chas, beloved sister of mine," Hope had finally said after a long argument, "my tush is out the studio door. My job is seeing that the contestants are interesting and that they appear. I can't help it if Ginger got married last night—this is a live show, Chas—have a heart . . . I've got to pull a sexy blonde out of some closet and you're the only live body I've got to work with. You could have a shape, I guess . . . with a real effort—if we worked with your . . ."

At this point, she had examined Chastity from head to toe, then continued with a frown. "You need makeup, a haircut and lightening, decent clothes, coaching in how to talk and walk, and voilá, a Heartbeat Goddess is born."

Hope had paused, scanned Chastity's loose, earth-colored clothing and tightly braided hair, and scrunched her lids together. "We'll work hard on the body part. You're definitely not built long and lean," she muttered quietly. "Thank God, you don't have to wear glasses for distances." Then she had opened her eyes slowly, smiled sweetly and played her trump card. "I know you love to putter in files and grow plants and all that boring stuff that makes you what you are—sweet. I know you like blah clothes and quiet and I love you with all my heart, Chas . . . but if you don't help me, I could lose a job that is making my career—change that—my *life,* amount to something. I'll make it up to you, I promise . . . trust me. I'll love you forever," she had said as Chastity groaned loudly.

In the end, Chastity submitted as she had always done in the face of Hope's disasters.

Then there was the matter of the thousand dollars, which would help clear her mother's last credit card mess. Grace

Beauchamp's addiction for ordering television bargains was momentarily under control; however the credit card bills remained, with a sum due on Chastity's grandfather's nursing-home tab.

From the Big Pool Hall in the Sky, the Old Coot's chuckle floated over Chastity. Her grandfather had loved a good con game.

Chastity closed her eyes, aching for her grandfather. As a child, she ran to the Old Coot for love while her mother flitted through affairs and loved the two children she'd had before Chastity. He insisted that she had inherited his special talent, giving her the identity she needed to survive in a hectic, Gypsy environment. Created "on the wrong side of the blanket" and ignored as a child, Chastity had always wanted someone to love who was hers alone—her special person who loved her with equal intensity.

Now Chastity stood waiting to be introduced on a show she never watched, primed with directions on how to be appealing and wishing she'd resisted her sister's final coup de grace, "Please don't cost me this job, Chas. It's my life. Oh, and don't tell anyone that we're related. It's a no-no on the show."

The long, slinky earrings in Chastity's ears slithered against her neck, tangling in the wealth of newly lightened hair that reached her midback. In the dressing room mirror, her shadowed and mascaraed eyes had seemed enormous. Hope had used cosmetics and brushes like an artist until a gorgeous, sexy blonde named "Honey" had emerged.

Lyle Drake introduced Honey, and a roar of catcalls and whistles shot up from the studio audience. Chastity swallowed and reminded herself to walk slowly toward the host. Then Lyle's firm hand enclosed hers and she returned his warm smile, forcing herself to forget her new tight lingerie, which did unearthly, spectacular and pert things to her bosom.

The "Heartbeats" host drew her to the two chairs on-stage. "Honey is gorgeous, candidates behind the curtain. She's everyman's dream. Our last winner, Ginger, was unable to play at the last minute and we were lucky to find Honey. As you know, the show's format is that the contestant who is chosen this time will ask the questions on the next show. He or she returns from their exciting weekend, shares the fun with the audience, and then chooses a date-mate from a new contestant line-up, allowing the show to continue. Make no mistake, gentlemen behind the curtain, Honey is a knockout, not second choice in any dating book. Come on, Honey, tell us a little about yourself—what's your job, what you do for fun—something to give those guys behind the curtain and our audience a little insight to the real you. For instance, why did you want to appear on 'Heartbeats'? Come on, Honey, sit down..."

Blinded by the lights, Chastity focused on Hope's directions. *Follow Lyle's lead. Read my questions and "ooze" remarks like, Oh, I'd love to share a midnight dinner with you....*

She repeated the breathless, sexy "Hi, Lyle" Hope had designed, and tried to equally lift the corners of her mouth. Hope had forced her to practice equalizing her smile until her cheeks ached. Lyle was a nice man, according to her sister; he needed the show's high ratings to help provide for his three small children. "Lean on me, kid," he had said in their preshow interview. "It's just a game, and you're perfect for the part. Hope sure knows how to pick 'em. Loosen up, it's just for fun and we're glad you're helping us by filling in."

"Well, Lyle," she murmured slowly, huskily after dampening her lips for the cameras and bringing up that reluctant left corner of her mouth. "I work in an office. Right now, I'm in-between on the dating scene, and there are no significant others. I just love this show. I watch it every day, so do my friends."

Between dates? Chastity winced inwardly, then decided
the statement was true. Randall had been a steady date for
a year... two years ago. In the future, she hoped to have
another date.

An expert host, Lyle snared her hand and held it reassur-
ingly. "You're gorgeous, Honey. To El Toro, Dream Guy
and the Love Bandit behind the curtain, Honey is about five
foot six inches tall, a leggy, green-eyed blonde with a very
cuddly look. She's in her twenties and has never been married. Tell us what you're looking for in a weekend date, that
special something that interests you."

Behind a studio camera Hope licked her lips, silently in-
structing Chastity to do the same. *"Move sensual, sis. Move
like you were silk sliding on silk, like every pore of your
body enjoys being a woman who attracts men's stares...."*

Chastity smiled gently at Lyle. She carefully tilted her
head to one side, allowing a jumble of honey-colored curls
to flow across her bared shoulder. She rotated that shoulder slowly, picturing silk on silk, then answered softly in her
normal husky, hesitant tone, "I want a man who enjoys
spending lots of quiet time with me. One who doesn't need
a crowd to make him happy."

Lyle's eyebrows lifted. "I know *I'd* want to be alone with
you, Honey," he returned with a boyish grin that had
charmed her in their interview earlier. "Whoops. I didn't
mean that, Barbara," he said, waving to his wife at home.

Handing Chastity a gold box filled with twenty golden
hearts, Lyle said, "Let's get started, Honey. For every answer that appeals to you, drop a heart into the tube marked
El Toro, the Love Bandit or Dream Guy. The dateable delectable receiving the most gold hearts on this special Valentine show is your date for that weekend at Casa Bianca.
Now, what's your first question for our contestants?"

Honey glanced down at Hope's list of questions for the
contestants. If she had been drafted, the least she could do
was save Hope's job and Lyle's ratings. "I'd love to know

what each guy would want to do on our first date." She spaced her words slowly, deliciously apart, just as Hope had directed.

Lyle relayed the question to El Toro, who returned suggestively, "Honey, I'd do anything you want."

The audience cheered, and then Dream Guy launched into a lengthy list of a candlelight dinner, a bearskin rug and a hot tub.

The Love Bandit cleared his throat after a lengthy silence. "Maybe a movie. Maybe a dinner later...." The slow, deep drawl intrigued Chastity. The man was reluctant. If she *had* to spend a weekend with a dateable, she preferred a really reluctant man. She dropped a heart into Bandit's tube.

She asked the next question. "Describe what you think you do best...."

El Toro and Dream Guy giggled and joked and suggested a smorgasbord of delights. Chastity found she enjoyed the light banter with the two men. Her masquerade as a stunning blonde had become a game... like playing a Cinderella role. Her friends would never guess her identity—who would know she was just plain old Chastity from Charlie's Auto filing-and-bookkeeping department?

She licked her lips appropriately, adjusted her newly sensual body to the chair and crossed a length of bare thigh. She winked at Hope, whose mouth gaped.

Bandit hesitated again. Then his deep, liquidy voice, marked by a distinct twang, said, "Listening ... maybe."

Leaning forward, Chastity found herself waiting for that cowboy twang. *If* she had to spend a weekend with a dateable to preserve Hope's job, she wanted a man who wasn't primed for— "Listen to what, Bandit?"

The silence stretched into two heartbeats. "Listen to the rain. Listen to the wind moving through the grass. Listen to the old windmill catching the wind, moving with it." He was quiet, then said, "It's important to listen to people. Not what they say... but what's inside...."

Lyle made an impatient movement as though the cowboy's answers didn't fit the show's format, but Chastity listened, entranced. The man's wistful, lonely tone struck something soft and cuddly and feminine within her; she wanted to snuggle on his lap and— Lyle glanced closely at Chastity's expression and interrupted. "Bandit, tell Honey and the audience how you would like to kiss her the first time."

A chair scraped immediately behind the curtain and a man's low, dangerous tone snapped, "First, I'd ask if the lady wanted to."

Dream Guy added quickly, "Hot. I'd kiss her hot."

El Toro chimed in, "The neck . . . I'd start there. Women love it." He entered into a long dialogue with Dream Guy filled with innuendos.

"Where would *you* start, Bandit?" Chastity found herself asking. Parts of her body were heating, shifting and reassembling into one big question mark. Her feminine molecules anticipated Bandit's answer. The audience leaned forward in their seats. Chastity took a deep breath and closed her eyes, then licked her lips, almost tasting the cowboy's mouth.

"Depends, I guess," he returned in that soft, low drawl.

"On what?" she asked, aware that her breathing was uneven. "And where?"

"The lips, ma'am," the cowboy said as though speaking to a slow-witted child.

"I like kissing lips," Chastity said slowly, thoughtfully. She pictured a curvaceous blonde with mounds of curling hair snuggled to a tender cowboy's tall muscular length, held gently in his arms as he bent to kiss her. The romantic scene caused her to shiver, anticipating the man's mouth. She dropped five gold hearts into Bandit's tube and repeated Lyle's question. "Tell me how you would kiss me the first time, Bandit."

Chastity blinked, suddenly aware of how much she fitted into the role of Honey. *Lord, she wanted that cowboy's kiss.*

There was a muffled noise as the man cleared his throat. Then Bandit said uneasily, "Soft. I'd see if you...how you felt. What you smelled like up close.... Just soft," he finished impatiently.

In the audience, women sighed dreamily. Lyle squeezed Chastity's hand, his expression urging her to pursue the cowboy. "What do you think I smell like, Bandit?"

Again, the answer was deliberate, as though he'd thought about her scent. "Sweet. Like raindrops on..."

Chastity could sense him seeking the appropriate word. His sincerity and thoughtfulness was endearing.

"Like roses," Dream Guy supplied in an aside.

"Like orchids," El Toro muttered impatiently.

"Like raindrops on the spring prairie wind," Bandit finished firmly and the women in the audience went wild.

"Whew! What do you have to say about that, Honey?" Lyle asked with a grin that said: *Zinger. Ratings are up.*

Chastity sensed the camera sliding in for a close-up. She disregarded everything but her blatant attraction for Bandit. For him she wanted to be gorgeous and sexy and inviting. She maneuvered through a series of questions to the men and decided that El Toro and Dream Guy should be tossed back in elementary school, while Bandit was certified "Adult Male, Thoughtful and Sweet."

While the other men might need leashes at Honey's bedroom door, she was positive that Bandit would not place one boot over the threshold unless properly invited.

"I want him," she whispered firmly to Lyle, whose eyebrows shot up. The show's format called for more questions. She dumped the entire box of tiny gold hearts into Bandit's tube. "*I want that man.*"

Lyle stared blankly at her and "Honey" fluttered her lashes back at him. For good measure, she found Hope hovering behind the cameras and she fluttered Honey's lashes again.

If she was bound for a weekend with a man, she wanted a real one. A reluctant one with a slow, sensual cowboy drawl. She dismissed a weekend with the raging hormonal boys who needed shots.

Lyle chuckled and beamed. "Honey isn't a woman to waste words. She wants her luxurious weekend in Casa Bianca to be spent with...the Love Bandit," he announced happily. "Honey, let's meet the men you turned down—El Toro and Dream Guy."

Each man cuddled and kissed Chastity playfully. "And now...the Love Bandit," Lyle exclaimed jubilantly. The crowd cheered and Chastity's heart pounded heavily. She took a deep, uneven breath and waited....

The Love Bandit was gorgeous...tall and tasty. He was worth every gold heart on earth.

He walked toward her in a lithe, slow stride, all angles and reluctant masculinity. There were broad shoulders, gleaming blue-black hair, a vast chest tapering down to long legs sheathed in new jeans.

Western jeans, she noted with a burst of joy, not the designer brands, but the kind that fitted and molded—

Chastity inhaled sharply, ignoring the restricting cloth over her bosom and the way her breasts pushed upward. She gripped her hands together to keep them from reaching toward him.

She closed her lids, relishing the sight of Bandit behind them. She sighed and knew that his wary, don't-touch-me-ma'am look was hers to unravel over one entire, blissful weekend. Bandit was the present of her lifetime and she wanted to experience every little masculine angle—

Just once she wanted to reach out and take something really nice from life and, without doubt, Bandit was that special gift.

Her heart thumped wildly as her eyes slowly ran down his lean body, then traveled upward with absolute delight.

"Oh," she breathed unevenly, drawing Lyle's quick scrutiny. But "Honey" didn't care; she was too busy picturing the cowboy walking toward her wearing nothing but an overnight beard and a towel around his hips. Then she debated jerking the towel away, and whispered a soft "Oh" again.

Bandit hesitated warily, his legs locked at the knee as though he were a gunfighter sizing up dangerous territory. Then he breathed deeply and a muscle moved in his jaw as though he was gritting his teeth. Two tiny indentations appeared in his cheeks, indicating dimples. With grim control he walked toward her, his eyes narrowing on her face.

Chastity sensed Bandit's determination to keep his eyes above her bare shoulders and found that rather endearing.

She wanted to melt into him . . . wanted to curl against his six-foot-three rangy frame.

Honey wanted to stand on tiptoe, even in her stiletto heels, lift her mouth to Bandit's hard one and let him demonstrate the promised soft kiss. She was on a tight time frame and needed to snare his interest quickly, if she was to experience the cowboy's attentions.

Acting on impulse, Chastity sidled Honey's leggy, shapely body into the rangy cowboy's path, planting her curves firmly against his hard, delectable body. Mere inches from her, he remained gorgeous without the aid of her glasses. His thighs were hard and he smelled like soap and lime-scented after-shave.

Chastity fluttered Honey's lashes up at Bandit, tipped her head back and lifted her full, glossy lips invitingly.

Before her lids closed, Chastity saw the dark heat in Bandit's blue eyes. She saw the tightly leashed hunger and knew that he'd never take anything she didn't want to give. She adored the deepening, serious line between his well shaped eyebrows. Bandit had refused the show's makeup artist, the lines on his tanned face endearing.

Wrapped in the safety of his gentlemanly manners and Honey's sexy blonde image, Chastity placed her hands on his chest, her fingertips exploring the heavy pads of muscle.

They rippled. Hard cords shifted uneasily beneath her touch and Chastity stared up into Bandit's eyes as her hands floated over the width of his shoulders.

The heat and hunger flared in those dark blue eyes, and she sensed that this was the kind of man who'd pick her up and carry her off—if he were hers. Chastity had dreamed about this man, waited for him, and now he was within her grasp. She'd waited years to taste delight, and now...

Honey wanted to rip off his sweater and shirt and— Chastity blinked. Bandit smelled the way a man should, like soap and low-key after-shave. "You may kiss me, Bandit," she whispered huskily.

"Now, ma'am?" he asked politely, though a flush moved higher on his tanned cheeks. There was an arrogant tilt of his head as though he didn't bend easily. "We're on television...live."

She noted clean waves of hair, the way it just touched his collar. She touched the strands gently, noting with satisfaction that it was naturally crisp. Bandit was a very natural man. A touchable man. One that Honey could cuddle near, and nibble on his ear— Chastity noted the said earlobe. It did look tasty, dark and sweet and vulnerable. "Now, babe," she urged in Honey's husky, sultry tones.

He inhaled sharply, his eyes darkening dangerously. The cowboy was an exciting man with little masculine switches that she ached to flip on. She was pleased with the way she'd tossed the in-word, "babe," at him, thus proving that "Honey" knew how to play.

Chastity decided that there were certain advantages in acting the role of a vamp. She could step out of her shy character and grasp what she wanted—and *she wanted to experience that cowboy*. Beneath his sexy trappings, Bandit wore the wary look of a man who had tasted life and found it sour. Poor man, he needed a tender touch.

Bandit's jaw clenched and lowered into his collar. The grim curve of his hard mouth served as an obligatory smile.

Why wasn't he taking advantage of the moment? What was wrong with her, anyway? She'd taken hours preparing for the moment, including a drastic forty-eight-hour diet-and-exercise plan, and now Bandit wasn't all that eager. Maybe he preferred brunettes or redheads with evenly matched smiles....

Piqued by the brunettes and redheads clustering in Bandit's future, she whispered, "Sweetcakes, the audience is expecting you to kiss me. Do it."

Bandit wasn't just another pretty young cowboy. Anger rippled beneath the surface; his body heat snared her though he hadn't touched her. Blue-black eyebrows and lashes shielded deep set eyes; his squarish jaw bore the tinge of a recently shaved, but heavy beard.

Then there was just the cutest little tuft of black hair at his open collar. Chastity wanted to nuzzle her nose in the fresh soap and male scents.... "Later, ma'am. If it's all the same to you," Bandit said in a low aside.

Lyle took Chastity's hand to draw her away from Bandit. She looked longingly back at the man who moved to her side. He felt so good, standing there, firm and strong, that she leaned a little his way.

Because he was obviously a gentleman, Bandit's arm slid around her waist to support her. She snuggled back against him, enjoying the wealth of taut muscles and clean masculine scents.

A small shudder rippled through his tall length and for just an instant his fingers tightened on her waist, drawing her nearer. Chastity nestled against his hard frame, feeling like a cat who was being petted.

Chastity smiled at Lyle as he described the weekend at a posh resort near Las Vegas. But she was concentrating on Bandit's warm, hard thigh pressing against her backside as the host urged them closer to the other contestants on the stage. She barely heard the final chorus—behind her hips, Bandit's body had responded blatantly to her femininity. After all the insecurities of her lifetime, the cowboy's response was sheer glory. To let him know she appreciated the compliment, she lifted Honey's sultry hot look and traced his rugged features.

Bandit's mouth tightened, and her ego soared higher. For the moment, plain Chastity Beauchamp was disturbing a fantastic man and loving it.

Then Hope was hugging her and staring adoringly up at Bandit. The tall cowboy's brows were drawn fiercely together. He nodded to Chastity politely. "The name is Walkington, ma'am," he said stiffly. "Lucas Walkington. I reckon you're stuck with me for the weekend."

Hope blinked and gaped when Chastity leaned toward Lucas, licked her glossy lips and said, "You got it, sweetcakes. You and me. Together for one heck of a weekend."

"Chas, the man is dynamite. He is such a babe! He's got that untamed cowboy look, like he's been around and wary. Just the kind of man that a woman wants to...oh, you know."

Chastity adjusted her glasses and groaned. Bandit had made her feel just that way. Then Hope continued, "I can't believe how good you were on the show. They put three extra operators on the switchboard. The sponsors want a special show when you come back. They're talking about keeping the audience on hold for one whole month, *then* bringing you and Bandit back to the show. They think there was so much steam between you that, given a month, no telling what could happen!'' Hope almost crowed.

She drew a black lacy peignoir from the mound of clothes on Chastity's bed and folded it into a suitcase with the air of a general packing war missiles. ''There might not be any other games for you and Bandit. Everything just clicked right the first time. You'll cinch this week's ratings. The way you looked up at him and the way he— You sizzled, Chas. Everything is perfect. The audience feedback slips asked if there was a fan club for Lucas.... Trust me, you'll enjoy this weekend.''

''I don't know what came over me. I must be having an identity crisis, and it's your fault, Hope,'' Chastity said as she stared at the clothing Hope had selected. The skimpy black maillot suit was sinful, and one tiny strap supported the sequinned hot pink sheath. The dress represented her emotions when she'd seen Bandit, wary and tough, all broad shoulders and narrow hips.

She'd wanted to pet him, to snuggle against him, to wrap herself along that tall, hard body. Her trademark restraint had snapped and crumbled like a thin cracker. The green light inside her body had flipped on and she wanted whatever time she could pilfer alone with him. She wanted a time and a man of her own, unrestricted by the needs of other people. She wanted to bask in the fire and the hunger in those sky-blue eyes, to tuck reality under a sofa cushion and run with the excitement racing inside her.

Chastity watched as Hope added musk-scented bath salts to a bulging cosmetic bag and said quietly, ''I am sick.''

''No time for that, Chas. Sorry. The show's limo will be pulling up with Lucas in about fifteen minutes.''

"I don't know what came over me...why I let you or any of the family get me into these things," Chastity returned firmly while Hope fluffed her jumble of blond curls with a hair pick and adjusted the collar on her jumpsuit. "It's Friday night and I usually watch television and water my violets. Maybe repot a few plants. Filing is nerve-racking, you know, and auto payments must be entered properly. I'm under immense pressure every day, and Friday is my night to relax."

She breathed deeply and glared at Hope. Born after her mother's divorce from Hope and Brent's father, Chastity had always tucked her needs away and cared for theirs. With the one devastating lapse of claiming the cowboy for her own, she had never been greedy. "I've just recovered from getting our brother off the hook. Playing an irate wife isn't easy. Brent should have picked up his dog without the elaborate scene. I'm sure his ex-girlfriend really didn't want his Saint Bernard. Pickles eats a ton. Now you've got me flying off to Las Vegas for a weekend with a man I don't know. Have you noticed that cowboy's hat never falls off, never tips unless he adjusts it? I think there is something genuinely suspicious in that."

Hope ran a cosmetic brush filled with blush powder across Chastity's cheeks and studied the effect intently. "They learn that in cowboy school.... Use the Autumn Mauve shade to give that hollow look, Chas.... You're going to have a great time. Trust me. Just act like you did on the show—"

"I'm not a Heartbeat Goddess, not even close. Honey just isn't me," Chastity said between her teeth. "I just got caught up in the moment, that's all. Playing the part you and Brent cast me in as usual.... This is the last time you are going to get away with—"

"You look hot," Hope returned gleefully, lowering the jumpsuit front zipper two inches. She snatched Chastity's glasses away and repeated, "Real hot."

Two

At ten o'clock that night, Lucas sat watching Honey's progress back to their secluded, candlelit table. He had the sinking feeling that he'd been transported into another galaxy.

Casa Bianca lay miles from Las Vegas, a posh getaway that specialized in romance. The roomy suite he shared with Honey contained a private kitchen, stocked with exotic food for those who wanted absolute privacy. That tiny refrigerator held costly food worth more than several months of his grocery bills. A Jacuzzi with tropical plants and redwood decking sprawled just beyond a sunken living room, which held a fireplace.

Honey moved toward him in the nightclub, drawing male attention like bees to blossoming field clover, and he thought how she belonged in the exotic setting.

Her gold lamé top and slacks shimmered in the dim light. The top was magically supported by a single strap running around her delectable neck. Honey was all woman, her small waist and full bosom matching her soft hips. Beneath the slinky cloth of her slacks, her thighs moved strongly and Lucas found himself gritting his teeth. Drawn to the luscious curves and daring outfit, men traced her path, and Lucas pushed down his irritation as she approached.

He was too old for the reaction he'd had on "Heartbeats."

If ever Lucas read invitation in a woman's eyes, he found it in Honey's. A froth of blond hair tumbled from combs that pulled it back from her face, enlarging those huge green eyes.

He gripped his thigh hard beneath the tablecloth to remind himself that he wasn't a boy. Honey issued big welcoming signs at every look, every touch.

Lucas pressed his lips together. He might be over-the-hill about the rules of today's dating games, but he wasn't prepared for the open invitation. Honey smiled in that secret way of hers, just the right side of her mouth moving slightly, and Lucas studied those full, glossy lips.

He wondered briefly how many men had kissed that satin-soft, lush contour. With little effort, he pictured what Honey would look like after making love—drowsy, warm, cuddly. Just the woman to make a man forget mortgages, daughters that needed college funding and a ranch that never ran out of problems.

Here he was, lounging around at eleven o'clock on a Friday night, preparing to dance until dawn. The idea grated. A hardworking man, Lucas couldn't reconcile the loss of time and money while indulging himself.

Honey may be used to exotic retreats, but he hit the sack early and got up with the chickens....

As she approached the table he stood and drew her chair back for her to sit down. She glanced up at him appreciatively, the big green eyes dark as jade. "Thanks, Lucas."

He nodded curtly. That hesitant, sultry tone slid right into his stomach with the impact of a satin sledgehammer. He had signed an agreement to see the date through and he would. Lucas sat slowly, fitting his length into the chair and stretching his legs out under the table.

"Lucas?" Honey stretched out her soft hand to rest on the back of his. Her nails were long and bright red, expensive-looking like the rest of her. "Are you tired? Should we go back to the suite?"

Because he wasn't ready to share living space with a woman who looked incredibly soft and warm, Lucas shifted uneasily. The whirlwind trip from Tulsa to Chicago after a night of rescuing his cattle from a sudden late-spring snow didn't leave him much control. When Honey inhaled on "Heartbeats," her pale breasts had lifted upward, the softness had quivered with her pulse—a pulse that would run deep in her warm, curved body—and he'd had to force his eyes away. She seemed oblivious to the way her arms squeezed against the fullness as she stared hungrily up at him. A man would have to be stone-cold dead not to notice those eyes, and that irritated him. "I thought the schedule said dancing until dawn. The photographers will want to start shooting at ten in the morning."

Honey's low laughter stroked him like warm velvet. "Some relaxing weekend. We're scheduled every minute."

A man with spiked hair and loose clothing came up to their table, smiling at Lucas and Honey. He nodded at Honey and asked, "Dance?"

Lucas took a deep breath, unaccustomed to the freedom of one man to poach outright on another. He listened to the fast beat of the band and recognized it as a favorite song of his daughters. He'd been forced into learning the steps when they primed him for the Lonesome Cowboy contest. He glanced at Honey. "Dance with him if you want."

Her fingers tightened on his hand and somehow he found himself turning his palm and opening to her touch. When he'd sensed she needed him on the show, leaning against him, he'd responded the same immediate way. Despite her now-woman attitude, Honey had a shy turn to her that Lucas found appealing. She glanced at the man and shook her head. "I'm saving myself," she said huskily, indicating Lucas.

Lucas wondered darkly how many times a woman like her saved herself. The phrase "once in a blue moon" came to his mind.

He allowed himself to hold that soft hand within his, and instinctively ran his thumb across her palm. The tiny calluses surprised him.

The band swung into a slow tune and Honey looked at him. "Dance, cowboy?"

"Sure." He didn't bother with the line about stepping on her toes. He'd been doomed since his daughters had entered him in that first contest. Lately, he learned to take his medicine without fighting.

On the tiny floor, Honey moved into his arms as though she'd been there many times. Her arms slid up his chest to encircle his neck and she smiled that soft, one-sided, wistful smile up at him. "You look tired and grim, Lucas. I hope I'm not too much of a burden...."

He concentrated on moving his feet, carefully placing his hands on the small waist that flared into soft hips. He liked a woman with hips, he decided, smoothing the rounded curve. He tried not to think of her breasts nestled against his stomach.

Honey's soft arms tightened and her palm stroked his neck. "You're so stiff, Lucas." She gently massaged the taut cords at the back of his neck, toying with longish strands of hair that curled at his collar. She eased her cheek to his chest and turned her face against his throat. "I love to dance like this, don't you? It's so sweet."

"Sweet," he repeated grimly as her lips brushed his throat. His body wasn't remembering his age, the fact that he had jumped into his daughters' dare with both boots on, trying to placate the tortuous female mind—

Her hair brushed his cheek. Unlike her peers' teased and sprayed stiff curls, Honey's was soft and fragrant. Just the texture a man wanted sharing his pillow....

He glanced down and found his gaze locked to the crevice running between her full and half-exposed breasts. He wondered instantly how they would feel pressed against his bare chest or filling his hand. Forcing his lids closed, Lucas sensed the sweat beading his forehead. He was too old, too worn, and should have more control over his body when it came to women.

His body wasn't taking orders when Honey was near. The thought angered him. He should be long past the age when a woman's come-on could send him over the edge.

"Hold me close. I like being cuddled," Honey murmured against his throat.

"You're plenty close enough," Lucas returned roughly.

She glanced up, wide-eyed. "Touchy, sweetcakes. What's wrong?"

He studied the skillfully applied cosmetics intently before looking over her hair. Beneath the makeup, Honey's features were even, but not beautiful. Her walk and smile and the mysterious look in her sea-green eyes, as if she were waiting just for him—probably for any man—were designed to raise steam. "You wouldn't understand, but where I come from there are still times when a man makes the first move."

Her eyebrows lifted. "Really? When are you making yours?"

He chewed on that, taking her wrists away from his chest and leading her off the dance floor. "I think we're both tired. You can stay here and dance, or you can let me take you back to your... our room... our suite." He hoped she didn't see his face warm in the dim light.

"You're blushing, Lucas," she whispered softly, then ran a fingertip down his cheek. "That's cute. Let's go to *our* suite. You'll feel better after a night's rest." With that Honey turned slowly, shot him a sizzling look over her bare shoulder and winked. He was left to follow in a wake of admiring gazes.

Lucas frowned at her swaying hips. Honey moved in a leggy, smooth stalk that molded the gold fabric to her round hips. Lucas dried his palms against his pants.

He cursed silently as they moved through the foyer and Honey took his hand She was one touchable woman and a woman who liked touching. The muscles on his neck ached from stress—he was too old not to know the consequences of having his emotional cage rattled.

Honey liked to rattle cages, he thought darkly as she lifted her hand to ease away a curl from her cheek. The movement brought the gold cloth to her breasts, taut as it stretched from tip to tip within the folds.

A businessman in a suit stared at her, his expression showing clearly that he envied Lucas. He raised his thumbs upward in a way-to-go-guy signal and winked.

Honey leaned against Lucas and lifted her face to whisper, "They take terrible care of their plants here. They need repotting."

"Uh-huh," he returned as two men dressed in swimming trunks and towels stared openly at Honey. He nodded to them and noticed that one exhaled, letting his stomach return to its normal paunch.

In the suite, Lucas loosened his collar and opened the patio door to breathe the fresh night air. He should be sleeping now, or working on bills, choosing how much to what creditor. Instead he was thinking of Honey's wide green eyes and long legs.

He was thinking that maybe a man deserved a little soft skin and sweet perfume after years of loneliness. "Heartbeats" required a television rehash after the date, but then he'd never see her again—

Honey's perfume filled the air before her hand touched his back and stayed there. She rubbed his shoulder slowly. "It's only a weekend, Lucas. Try to enjoy yourself, okay? See you in the morning." With that she reached up to pat his cheek. "Sleep tight babe."

Lucas wanted to sleep tight. Or rather sleep tightly with— He forced his thoughts away from Honey's closed bedroom door and the circular bed with pink satin sheets.

Determined to shuck Honey for the night, Lucas lay full length on his bed and telephoned his ranch. While he was playing at Casa Bianca, the twins could be playing, too.

Lucas listened intently to the sound that had wakened him before dawn. "You're on the prowl pretty early for a city girl, aren't you, Honey?" he asked.

"How did you know that I was here?" she returned huskily from the terrace door.

He turned slowly on the black satin sheets, taking care to cover his hips. As experienced as Honey appeared to be, he didn't want to share evidence of his desire. Standing outlined in the predawn light and a filmy peignoir, Honey's curvaceous body did little to calm an uncomfortable problem that had kept him from sleeping. He yawned and stretched, unable to see her face in the shadows. "I knew you were here when the door latch clicked and your scent filled the room."

The lacy black peignoir floated around her as she moved toward him. She wrung her hands when she stopped at his bedside. "Lucas, we need to talk."

"What about?" He wondered then what that soft body would look like curled between the black satin sheets....

"What's wrong with me? You seem angry that I chose you...."

His thoughts erupted. "I'm a plain-speaking man, Honey. You might not like what I have to say."

"Really?" The tone challenged, and because Lucas was feeling raw, he saw no reason to shelter her.

"I'm thirty-eight, not some kid out on the prowl. You must be a good ten or so years younger than I am—"

"I'm thirty-four, sweetcakes," she returned sharply, plopping down on the bed. In a huffy movement, she gathered the peignoir around her like a queenly cape. She leaned closer and peered down at him closely. "Try again. Why are you so determined to be Mr. Meatball?"

"Mr. Meatball?" he repeated darkly. Didn't the lady know better than to enter a man's bedroom in the early morning and start tossing taunts at him? He jerked a black-satin-covered pillow to the headboard and propped himself against it. "Listen, lady, I've got a dry ranch back in Oklahoma and two seventeen-year-old daughters who are trouble with a capital *T. What I am not, is a fun date.* Sorry, but you picked the wrong man for games. It goes against my grain to be bought with twenty little gold hearts like some yahoo with no sense. I'm long past this—" He paused, debated the word, and said, "Manure."

"You're thirty-eight, a rancher, and you're determined not to have fun, is that the picture, babe?" she challenged between her teeth.

The word "babe" threw him over the edge. He looped his fingers around her slender wrist and jerked slightly, unbalancing her. Another tug and she sprawled full length beneath him. He expected her to fight and covered her body with his, gripping her wrists in his hands. "You are going to listen to sense, lady...." he began, then realized that Honey wasn't struggling.

She lay looking up at him with those green eyes filling her pale face. In the shadows, her face was bare of cosmetics, her lips more soft and luscious than when covered with gloss. "This is what you want, isn't it?" he asked when he could speak.

Honey was soft in all the right places, he realized immediately. Every bit of her was real and womanly. "Damn," he said quietly, as his body went taut.

"Gracious," she returned in an uneven whisper, staring up at him. She blinked rapidly as though trying to focus better.

Cradled in her long legs, Lucas suddenly forgot his reasons for not wanting her. The heat burning through the cloth separating them had aroused him instantly. "I'm past the fun-and-games stage right now, I reckon."

She lifted her hips slightly, and Lucas pressed into the soft juncture instinctively. He yearned for a moment of primordial heat and passion that would warm the ache he'd carried for a lifetime. The moist aroused, feminine scent of her body swirled around him as she rubbed her thigh up and down his legs. "Reckon you are, babe," she murmured.

"Damn," he said again, fervently, as she grinned and repeated the enticing movement, the cloth between them dampening. "You are really asking for it."

Lucas could not stop tracing her lips. When he did stop, his gaze slid down to her breasts shimmering in a pool of black lace. He closed his eyes.

He'd been years without a woman's soft body, and now the need pushed violently at him.

Each breath raised her softness against him. Each time he breathed, he smelled her scent beneath the perfume. "You just took a bath," he murmured quietly, watching her. A ringlet coiled at her throat and he nuzzled it, smelling the shampoo and the soft skin beneath his lips.

"I'm a morning person, babe. I was too tired last night," she returned absently as she examined his face. "You look great in the morning."

Lucas felt eighteen again and about ten feet tall. "What about that kiss now?" he asked huskily, his fingers trailing down her arm to caress her side.

Lord, how he wanted to touch those soft breasts. How he wanted to taste and roll and— He inhaled sharply, fighting the stark desire. "Kiss me, Lucas," she invited softly, her hands framing his cheeks. "And make it good. I've waited a long time for a man like you."

He tried to think then, tried to make sense of her statement, but her hands were drawing his mouth to hers. . . .

Whatever Honey was, she was sweet to kiss, he thought as he tasted her mouth gently. He nibbled her bottom lip, moving slowly to the corners. Whatever she was, Honey made him forget everything but kissing her, feeling that soft womanly body cradle him invitingly.

She kissed like an innocent. Just the girl-woman that a man wanted to teach for him alone. Her hands smoothed his shoulders and his upper arms. After a long moment, he lifted his head to look down at her. In the dawn, he traced a pair of wide-set green eyes, drowsy with invitation. A bit of a nose preceded a generous, well-kissed mouth.

She made a purring noise that sounded like hunger, and he shifted slightly, pressing deeper into the juncture of her thighs. Satin and lace separated them now, and he could feel her heat, sense her waiting for him. "What do we do now?" she asked hesitantly.

Then her tongue licked her upper lip and Lucas tried to think of something cute. But all he could think was how much he wanted her wanted everything she offered, if only for the moment.

"One of two things, ma'am. You figure out which one and let me know. If you choose to stay in this bed with me, you'd better know that I'm not prepared—"

Her kiss sealed the rest of his words away forever. "I want you now, babe."

He studied her intent expression. "That might not be smart, but I haven't had a woman in a long time. We can wait until we've got protection, but you push me and—" Somehow it was important that he treat her honestly and gently.

"It's been a long time for me, too." She ran her cheek along his chest, nuzzling the crisp hair and kissing him. "My, you are tasty."

He chuckled. "'Tasty.' Don't remember ever being called that before."

She framed his jaw, nibbling at his mouth. "You're mine, Lucas Walkington. You smiled just then and showed me your dimples. That makes you mine for the weekend. Now make it count, will you, cowboy?"

Nothing could have stopped him, she met him kiss for kiss and then he was pushing against her heat— "What the—?"

Honey breathed quickly, her fingers pressing into his shoulder as she frowned up at him, her thighs quivering along his. "Ah . . . Lucas . . . are we having a problem?"

"Problem," he gritted, shaking with the need to enter her completely. He braced his weight on his hands, raising slightly. "You missed a minor detail, didn't you, lady?"

"Detail?" she asked too innocently, then swallowed. "Whatever could that be?"

"Sex," he stated flatly, thoroughly frustrated. His body shuddered, aching to slide deep into her moist depths. The tiny barrier and tight channel had surprised him. "You haven't had a man—ever."

She blinked, wincing slightly as he pushed gently to prove the point. "Of course. I know."

"Hell," he gritted softly as he lowered himself carefully to rest his head on the pillow beside hers. "Give me a minute...*and don't move...quit wiggling,*" he ordered against her throat.

"But, Lucas . . . I want you," she wailed softly, scooting closer.

"You shouldn't say things like that," he said tightly. "I don't want to hurt you."

"Sweetcakes, you and I both know there's no way to avoid it. It's just the first time and then we'll be fine."

He grinned ruefully, enchanted by the way she blithely dismissed her virginity and the way he felt as if some great honor had been bestowed upon him. "That's supposed to be my line, buttercup."

Her small "Oh, I didn't know" caused him to grin wider, despite the sensual urgency driving him.

She bristled slightly. "You can stop feeling superior. I would have sooner, but there wasn't anyone as appealing and it didn't seem worth the effort."

He chuckled, smoothing a long, soft expanse of trembling thigh. She wanted him badly and wasn't afraid to show it. Honey tugged on his chest hair, making him wince despite his utter happiness. "Stop making fun of me."

"I wasn't. A man likes to know he is appreciated. If you're serious, and I hope you are, lady. We'd better do this nice and slow."

Honey tugged him closer. "You're a great kisser. You probably do everything great. Lead on."

Another time, Lucas might have laughed outright. Just now he waited while Honey eased a little closer to him and said wonderingly, "My. Oh, my. Is this going to work?"

Lucas closed his eyes, straining for control. Whatever Honey was, she was sweet and fresh and wanting him. "Are you sure?"

"Sweetcakes, I've never been more certain of anything in my life."

Then he was in her, her soft cry taken by his mouth. He fought the desire taking him over the edge, waiting for her comfort. Then she was taking him further....

Chastity awoke to a gentle slap on her bare backside. Tangled with Lucas's big body on satin sheets was a perfect way to spend a Saturday morning. He was so cute, she decided drowsily as his fingers lingered to caress her hips, holding the softness in his palm.

Then in a quick movement that took her breath away, Lucas hauled her up and over him. She blinked again rapidly, trying to focus on his face. He stroked back a wispy tendril that clung to her cheek and he kissed her nose. "I don't suppose you'd like to explain what happened an hour ago. Why you decided to give me your virginity?"

Chastity kept her lids closed, wallowing in the warm, hard body beneath her and the feeling of being well loved. She squirmed slightly for comfort and grinned when Lucas responded magnificently. He was so sweet, a real Band-Aid on her deflated femininity. "I haven't seen anything appealing to date and I wanted you. What's hard to understand?"

"But the way you look, the way you flirt...a man thinks—"

"Mmm," Chastity squirmed around on the delectable surface that was suddenly tensing. "I think we should practice."

He caught her upper arms and lifted her slightly away. "Oh, no, you don't. You've just gifted me with something pretty special—"

Chastity smiled softly. "That's exactly why I picked you. You're sweet and caring, when you're not grim. I love the way you laugh like just before you slept—"

"Honey," Lucas said gently, kissing her chin. "There's no time—the camera crew will be here in ten minutes. You know this relationship can't go anywhere, don't you? I haven't a thing to offer you."

"Sure," she replied brightly, and a piece of her heart tore away. "It's just for the weekend."

Lucas sat on the edge of the pool and watched Honey walk toward him, the skimpy black maillot drawing interested male stares. The photographers had taken shots of them at their patio breakfast and in various poses lounging around the luxurious suite. At the poolside lunch, they'd requested Honey to sit on his lap and she'd obliged. The soft tangle of arms and legs and the lush contours snuggling against him set Lucas off like a shot.

He'd snapped at the photographers, and Honey had soothed the moment by kissing him. The long, sweet kiss pleased the cameramen and stopped him dead. Lucas didn't feel dead; he wanted to carry her off to a secluded nook and finish what she had started.

When the photographers asked him to oil her back, Lucas sat on the wide lounge beside Honey's stretched-out body and wondered how he was going to live until they were alone. Her sleepy, sated gaze up at him over her shoulder reminded him of her look earlier, after they'd made love.

Needing her near him, Lucas nudged her aside and settled down on his back.

Honey had snuggled to his side as though she belonged there and had nibbled on his shoulder when the photographers weren't looking. Her hand found his chest, stroking it, and Lucas dozed momentarily, placing his hand over hers. He awoke to a camera click and discovered his other hand resting possessively on the back of her thigh. The photographers leered when he cursed, and assured him that they couldn't use the intimate shot for the show, but that he might want the photograph for his "private collection."

Lucas snorted. As if he had a "private collection."

Now Honey glanced at him and blushed wildly before diving neatly into the pool. She swam a half length before she surfaced at his feet. She shook her hair from her eyes and grinned. She tickled his sole beneath the water and sunk to nibble on his toe, then emerged with an impish grin. "Miss me?"

From where he sat, Lucas had a full view of Honey's curves. He pushed back the thought that he hadn't taken time to explore and taste that lovely expanse of soft flesh. He still had the feeling of falling off the top of a windmill, with the ground far below.

At any moment there would be a rude, painful awakening.

Now Honey looked up at him with those wide, mysterious green eyes and blinked the water from her lashes. Her hands rested on his knees. "You're being grim again, cowboy."

"How do you feel?" he asked carefully, still unable to believe that she had chosen him.

"Like eating the whole evening buffet. Are we going dancing tonight at the club?"

"Uh-huh. Have to for the publicity shots. Ed and Jonesy are coming, too." He thought about that willing, tight little body beneath the maillot suit and groaned inwardly. "You ate enough breakfast for two people."

She wiggled her eyebrows lewdly. "Exercise, my good man. It makes me hungry."

He laughed outright. Whoever Honey was, she was good for his morale. "We're not exercising again like that until we're protected, woman."

Lucas touched her lashes, smoothing them dry with his thumb. Just after making love, he'd dozed for a moment and awoke with the certain knowledge that he'd given her a part of himself. The knowledge was elemental, something older than time, but the certainty was there—a part of him had become hers.

"Grr...you've got that closed-in, thoughtful look. I love it when you get all broody and possessive, cowboy," she teased with a grin.

He caught her wandering hand, drawing her up and out of the water. "I want you to spend time in the hot tub, Miss Sassy Mouth. That should take the ache out of—" He found himself floundering as her eyes widened and she began to giggle.

Lucas discovered that he could blush.

Later, as they were dressing for dinner, Honey called him from her bedroom. "Lucas, would you please come here?" Ed and Jonesy winked and fiddled with their camera equipment as he crossed the suite to her door.

He entered the all-pink room warily, then closed the door quickly when he saw Honey. Dressed in a lacy beige bra and panties that his daughters called "French-cut," Honey frowned at the pink sequin-studded garment in her hand. "The hem is coming out of this dress, and I really wanted to wear it. What else would look—" She turned to catch Lucas's hungry stare skimming down her body and added, "Talk about looks. You do things for a woman's ego, sweetcakes."

"They're doing publicity photos tonight, right?" he asked, knowing the answer and angry with himself for being out of control.

"Mmm. We have a minute or two. Do you know what I would like?" Honey began to walk toward him and Lucas's mouth dried, his body tensing immediately as she stopped near him.

"What?" he managed after clearing his throat.

Honey slipped her hands inside his shirt and gently tugged it open to reveal the hair on his chest. She nuzzled his skin. "We could hide."

"Can't. We both signed agreements, remember?" He allowed his hands to slide down her waist and rest on the curve of her hips. "Then, we'll have to improvise...." Honey looked at him hopefully.

He laughed outright, surprised to find himself so much at ease. "You're a scamp, Miss Honey. Reckon I could patch this bit of a dress for you."

"You? Patch? You're kidding." Within moments, Lucas was sitting on her bed, neatly mending the torn dress. He held it up for her inspection, tucked his needle in the traveling sewing kit and stood.

"Well, I'll be horn-swaggled," she said in an exaggerated Oklahoma drawl.

"Beats letting the commoners ogle your sweet hide, ma'am," he returned as she slid the dress over her head.

Before Lucas could move, Honey clicked the bedroom lock and leaped up on him, closing her long legs around his hips. The force of her body took him against the wall, and surprised, Lucas reached to support her body from harm. His palms cupped her lace-covered buttocks. Honey hugged his neck and kissed his cheek. "I knew you were special, Lucas, sweetcakes. How often can a cowboy patch clothes and carry his own little sewing kit?" she exclaimed in delight as she began kissing his mouth in hungry little pecks.

"Ma'am," he felt honor-bound to admit, "my daughters are seventeen. I've had to mend a time or two to keep them in clothes."

She snuggled closer, drawing him into a silky tangle of arms and legs and sweet perfume. "Oh, Lucas. You are wonderful. Do you know what I'd like you to do for me? Kiss my breasts, that's what. We never got around to that this morning, and you just seemed so upset and concerned, that I hated to ask. I really want you to— I'm aching to have your mouth there. Just *aching*, Lucas.''

Lucas stared helplessly up at Honey as she somehow levered her breast near his mouth. ''You can't wrinkle sequins. Look...'' She wiggled slightly and a thin strap slid down her shoulder.

''Do you realize how old I am?'' Lucas demanded when he could speak. ''Sure too old for games—'' But his hand tightened beneath her hips, smoothing the lush contour.

She nodded solemnly, her eyes dark green and mysterious. ''Is what happened this morning all there is, Lucas?'' she asked hesitantly, sadly.

''Honey,'' he began firmly, trying to dredge up all the reasons why they shouldn't play a weekend game that was destined for a dusty scrapbook.

Her legs tightened around his hips and Lucas shuddered, desperate for the taste of her skin. ''Oh, Lucas,'' she whispered unevenly as he nuzzled aside the lace to draw her breast gently into his mouth.

''Oh, Lucas,'' she repeated as he sensed her soft explosion, one that left her limply holding him. She snuggled against him, her heat enfolding them both in a tiny, private moment. He let her legs drift slowly to the floor, then picked her up and carried her to the bed.

Holding her on his lap, Lucas stroked and kissed until Honey stopped the gentle trembling. ''There's that, and more,'' he whispered gently into her ear and wondered dazedly how he was going to live until they were alone again.

Then Ed knocked on the door. ''Hey, our dinner reservations are for seven. Hurry up.''

Throughout the long evening, Honey's pink-sequin-covered body kept him on a constant alert. She snuggled to him on the dance floor, her expression that of absolute sensuality as she moved closer to him.

"Your chest is so hard, Lucas. I keep remembering—"
She stopped, swallowed and pushed her hot face into the
shelter of his neck and shoulders. She moved against him
and whispered in his ear, "I want you against me, holding
me, with nothing between."

Then she sighed wistfully and the sound went through
Lucas like the sweet spring wind sweeping the prairie clean.

Lucas closed his eyes and absorbed everything about
Honey right into his bones, because he knew dreams didn't
last.

Chicago dream girls and dirt-poor Oklahoma cowboys
didn't mix.

Three

———

Lucas slammed the posthole digger into the soft spring earth, pushed the handles together and lifted out a good chunk of Oklahoma sod. He hadn't slept for two weeks, his bed without Honey as welcoming as a cold rock shelf. Her sweet gasps of surprise had echoed from the last sound of the meadowlark until the morning dove began to coo.

He ran his forearm across his forehead, drying the sweat with his sleeve. He'd worked hard to forget Honey, to get her out of his blood, but she stuck in there; when he could manage to sleep, he awoke to empty arms and the hard reminder that once he'd been awakened by Honey's soft, warm body flowing on his.

She'd winded him, and again he was left feeling as though he'd given her a primordial essence, a tiny piece of himself.

New Angus calves gamboled around the cows, lending a timelessness to the land. Scanning the Oklahoma hills, Lucas concentrated on the rhythm of his neighbor's oil rigs, which stood on the horizon like huge chickens bobbing for grain. His grandparents were born in the Cherokee territory, before Oklahoma became a state. His great, great grandmother had survived the Trail of Tears. The solitude of the land was bred into him.

Honey was a creature of luxuries; her wardrobe alone cost more than his old barn. High heels and country dirt weren't a good blend. Toss in the old house, needing repair, and the antics of two daughters with just one year of high school left, and the situation would make a glamour girl turn tail and run for the nearest city.

He inhaled slowly. Honey was a special female, half girl and all woman. She deserved a man who could give her a good, comfortable life.

He'd tangled with love and dreams and come away with a bad taste in his mouth. Alesha had taken something from him, other than the first three years of his daughters' lives. She'd taken his pride, made him wary, bitter about women's needs, and made him ache every time he saw a boy marry his best girl. . . .

Summer and Raven rode toward him on spirited mares. His daughters knew how to ride, as graceful as Alesha. They slid from their horses before reaching a full stop. Dressed in sweatshirts and jeans, they bore the color and the lanky, tall Walkington build. "Hi, Daddy," they said in unison.

Raven handed him a cold beer from her saddlebag and grinned as he drank thirstily. Summer clasped her hands behind her and matched her twin's grin. Lucas glanced from one girl to the other, deeply pleased by the way they were stamped with Walkington height, black hair and blue eyes. Experienced with their antics, he asked, "What's up?"

"Nothing," Summer said too innocently, her blue eyes widening.

Raven, always more sensible glanced at her sister and plucked a stalk of dried range grass. "Daddy, we're fixing your favorite meat loaf for supper and scalloped potatoes and chocolate cake with fudge frosting. Summer has folded the laundry and we've cleaned all day—"

"Uh-huh," Lucas said warily. "I asked what's up?"

"Oh, Daddy, we want to go to Chicago with you to meet Honey," Summer burst out.

Lucas tossed the empty beer can to her and tugged up his leather gloves. "No."

Raven thrust her hands into her jeans, locking her long legs at the knee, her jaw set to challenge him. "Why not, Dad?"

There was that ruthless tone, the Walkington temper stored carefully away. Lucas plunged the posthole digger into the ground, reluctantly admiring the way the girls managed to stand up for what they believed. They'd inherited that much from him.

"She's special, Dad," Summer stated. "Honey's got something that makes you laugh. We saw it in the program and in those pictures the studio sent. You looked good together, Dad."

Raven grinned and teased, "Sweetcakes . . . Babe . . ."

"Shh. Show some respect," Summer ordered sharply and smothered her grin. "Dad may be just another 'Heartbeats' sweetcakes and babe, but he is our father." The twins began giggling, and launched themselves against him.

"Please, Daddy. Please call Honey. You saw her face on the videotape. She really liked you."

Disentangling himself from hugs and pleading blue eyes, Lucas stepped away. "None of that. It wouldn't work."

Lucas squinted against the bright afternoon sun and thought about the photographs hidden from his daughters. The one with him looking like one pleased hombre lying next to Honey's curvaceous backside, his dark hand on her soft pale thigh, was very private.

"Daddy, what Summer means is maybe you've been out of practice so long that, well . . . maybe we could help—"

"Lay off, girls. I'm not seeing her again after the last show. There's no point in it."

He wanted to remember Honey's last kiss, not her expression of disgust when she saw his ranch. Working at odd jobs around the country, he could manage to scavenge enough money to pay taxes and support his girls. Honey would want more—like water-demanding bubble baths, a lawn that was watered and green in the summer, and a man who could afford to take her out to dinner. Her long, pretty nails wouldn't last long without a dishwasher, and her sequins weren't meant to flap on a dry Oklahoma wind. Patched muslin sheets weren't pink satin, and his plain oak bed wasn't round.

"We'll be going away to college after this last year of high school, Dad. You'll be left alone. Mrs. Evans says hermits get sour, and now that we know you can get real . . . I mean have fun . . . I mean, act like a stu—" Summer stopped abruptly when he scowled at her.

Lucas threw the posthole digger to the ground forcefully and tipped his hat back. He glared at the girls who glared back, unfrightened. After a long moment, he said carefully, "Get this and get it good—Honey and I are not suited for each other."

"That's manure," Raven said with a tight smile meeting his hard stare. "You said the same thing about Wayne, our poodle, when those folks left him to bake in that deserted car. You broke the window, brought him home and made him ours. You threatened them with all sorts of things when they came to claim Wayne."

"Kaspar Percival Reynard de Montchamp? He's some ranch-yard dog, isn't he? Worthless piece of coyote. Cross between a curly coat lamb and a house cat."

"Daddy, he's *your* dog. He loves you better than us. Try again, Daddy," Summer said, bracing her long legs firmly into the Oklahoma sod as her ancestors had done.

"Okay, you're old enough to know why," Lucas said tightly. Since his daughters entered their teenage years, he had tried to cope with a realm of unsteady female emotions. He'd learned a couple of things as a single father: there were feminine cycles in which the girls either cried or raged, and his best safety was quiet. The other thing he'd learned was to spread his cards on the table and await the consequences. He'd discovered his daughters had a good sense of balance despite their years. "Honey isn't the kind of woman who could live on a ranch like this. I tried it once and it didn't work."

"Mother definitely is not country," Raven said thoughtfully, remembering her visits to Alesha's Tulsa home.

"Neither is Honey," Lucas stated firmly. He bent to pick up the posthole digger. "So lay off. Do whatever women do to get over the sulks. Raven, lay out your lacy blouse. I'll patch it tonight."

This time Raven wasn't to be bought off by mending. "Daddy, you're not using us as an excuse to hide from love. Something happened when you were with Honey and you've been molding away like a bale of hay in the rain."

Her twin looked straight into Lucas's dark face. "She's not Mother. Give it a chance or Raven and I will always feel to blame."

He knew better than to mix in matters better left alone, but that night Lucas dialed the home number that Hope had given him for emergencies. His fingers shook slightly, fear running wildly through him. He didn't have a lick of sense. Honey wanted him and against his better judgment, he'd initiated her into womanhood. A call to her could break up a romantic dinner....

Lucas's knuckles turned white as he gripped the telephone. The vision of Honey in another man's arms brought anger surging through him, hot and wild.

His stomach knotted painfully. Honey's current man probably could afford romantic weekends in posh resorts, his hands soft on Honey's silky skin—his heart kicked into double-time, pounding like a runaway horse.

Wayne rolled over, presenting his belly for Lucas's nightly toe-rubbing. Excitement quivered over the telephone lines as Hope directed his call to Honey's apartment.

The sweat on his forehead grew cold in his dark bedroom, the muscles in his jaw aching from tension. Taking a fierce, deep breath for courage, he punched out the buttons with one hand and crushed the lace blouse he'd been mending with the other. "Hello, dear heart," an older woman answered in a high, quivery voice.

Without pausing to allow Lucas to introduce himself, she began an involved explanation of why she had burned the soup. In the background, jazz played softly, liquid sloshed, and ice cubes clinked. Gracie, as she called herself, was "tibbling a bit after a bad day," and she was so happy he had called to chat. Her daughter, Chastity, was sleeping, and she, the mother, would take a message.

"Sachmo" revved up his horn as Grace described the horrendous red shade her beautician had chosen for her nails. Lucas sympathized on cue, sensing that when tipsy Grace could indulge tidbits about Chastity. Grace rambled through her family soup recipe, sipped her iced drink, then sighed. "I do hate this shade of red. Chastity seems so tired lately. Of course, I know that a pregnant woman usually just drops into bed almost immediately. Heavens, I wouldn't want to tell my own daughter that she's pregnant before she discovers it herself. That just wouldn't be right. But you know, I spent the first three months of my pregnancy with Chastity draped over every couch and chair I could find, if not a bed. She's got that pregnant look, but I should try a pink shade next time."

Gripping the telephone tightly, Lucas forced himself to breathe quietly while his heart thudded loudly. A shot of sheer pleasure raced through him as he remembered her body opening to his. "She's lucky to have you taking care of her," he murmured.

Grace was like a hungry trout leaping toward a fresh bug as she answered with the slightest "Yes, you're right." Lucas listened intently, forcing himself to breathe normally. "She sleeps—Lord, how that little girl sleeps. Poor thing, poor little innocent girl who went to Las Vegas with some hot-pants young two-by-four—they call them studs, you know. He just took advantage of my poor little plain girl, that's all. Left her in a terrible mess." Grace paused to munch on something crisp and swallowed.

Lucas lay back in his worn armchair, his eyes closed. "Honey" had been so eager, so new— The baby was his. *Baby.* His eyes opened as Grace rambled blithely on. "They ought to do something with those...boys before they allow them to escort ladies to these fancy resorts, you know. Something to drain off all that excessive sexual energy. There she was, alone without me, having to fend off that fiend...."

Hours later, Lucas inhaled the cold crisp midnight air. At thirty-eight, he was presented with a second round of fatherhood. He turned over the thought of a new baby, of the soft, desirable body sheltering it, and found himself grinning and glowing.

A truck's headlights soared through the night on the neighboring dirt road and Lucas scowled at the intrusion. Honey didn't have to have the baby...or if she did, she didn't have to keep it. The Oklahoma chill settled in his bones and ached. "Damn," he muttered quietly, striding to his corral to saddle his big bay gelding. He eased Duke out into the night, preparing to think through fate's newest present to him.

At a knoll overlooking his house, Lucas braced his forearms over the saddle horn. He'd taken pride in raising his daughters, giving them what he had and loving them. One good disaster could cost everything he'd worked to keep in his family.

He had his daughters and a fingertip hold on his life. Born and bred to Oklahoma dirt, he'd found sunshine for a few hours in Honey's arms.

Fear wasn't new to Lucas. He recognized the giant fist squeezing his entrails and panic pouring into his veins. There wasn't a chance in hell that Honey could be carrying another man's baby. *Damned if he ever wanted her near another man.*

If he had any horse sense at all, he'd leave her alone.

The Walkingtons never ran from trouble.

Honey wasn't trouble; she was soft and sweet—

Lucas forced himself to swallow. At twenty-one, he'd reached out and grabbed a dream. The shredded remnants left him living a nightmare, carrying enough guilt inside his gut to last an eternity. Without his girls, he wondered if he would have survived.

To go after what he so fiercely wanted this time was certain disaster.

The picture of Honey with a baby in her arms caught his breath. She was carrying his baby and no other yahoo was taking the right to see her through this away from him.

No other yahoo was sidling up to Honey and claiming her.

With grim determination, Lucas urged the horse to walk slowly back to the corral. Whatever happened, he was claiming the baby Honey carried as his responsibility. "Hotpants two-by-four," he muttered darkly as he unsaddled Duke and prepared for a long sleepless night.

The next morning, Summer's eyes widened over the breakfast table. "Dad? You're kidding."

He shrugged, cupping his coffee for warmth. When a man prepared to reach out and snag something good, he'd better lay a good foundation. He'd explained to his daughters as gently as possible, relying on their ranch training to complete the picture. "It's only a possibility. When I see her at 'Heartbeats,' I'll know."

"You're bringing her here," Raven said quietly, watching him.

"Yes," he said firmly, ignoring the twins' cheers. "If I can. If she's carrying my baby, she'll need rescuing from smog and that family of hers. Listening to her mother describe their family, I get the picture that Honey shoulders a heavy responsibility.... Sounds like their lazy backsides need kicking.''

''Go get her, Daddy. Do it,'' Summer said firmly as she washed her breakfast dishes and scooped her schoolbooks off the kitchen table.

''Things are tight enough,'' he pushed, watching the twins closely. ''There will be expenses—''

''Suits me,'' Raven said, joining her sister at the door. Then, in two steps, she flung herself at him, hugging him tightly. ''Go for it.''

''I'm talking marriage, tidbits,'' he said slowly, following their intent expressions. ''I'm old fashioned and it wouldn't do to have her here without marriage and my baby is bearing my name.''

The girls nodded solemnly.

Lucas fought the tears burning his lids, holding Raven tightly. ''She might not come. She might come, have the baby and take off. There are no guarantees for anything.''

He struggled with the words, his fear that Honey wouldn't want to see him, nor return to his ranch. ''It's hard out here. She's bred to city life. By this time, she may have figured out that a romantic setting can do a lifetime of damage.''

''You can handle it, Daddy. We'll help.''

When Lucas stood alone in the room, he inhaled sharply and watched the girls' old pickup truck soar down the dirt road. They were thrilled with the romantic idea of his capturing a city love.

He was flat-out scared. A thin pocketbook and hard times weren't much to offer a woman like Honey.

The proverbial limb to which he clung quivered threateningly. A second go 'round with a woman wasn't what he wanted.

Three weeks and two days after her beautiful weekend with Lucas, Chastity sipped her cup of jasmine tea and listened to Hope rave about Honey and the Bandit's ratings. On each ''Heartbeats'' show a fresh screen picture of Lucas and herself was presented, á la Ed and Jonesy, reminding her of that beautiful weekend.

The camera men had been ruthless in their pursuit, and when Chastity and Lucas were finally alone in their suite, she'd blown the whole evening by falling asleep on her bed. She had awakened to the delightful warmth of Lucas's bare body spooned against her back, his arm resting possessively across her waist. She loved nestling into the aroused male heat, loved his arm tightening around her.

She'd turned slowly to face a masculine confection of new beard and darkly tanned torso wrapped in pink satin sheets. He snored gently with a look of pure pleasure swathing his dark features. She couldn't resist sliding over him, joining sweetly with him as he slept and awakening him with nibbling kisses.

Clearly Lucas was having a delightful dream. He grinned sleepily and she caught his earlobe in her teeth. Then there was no time for anything but pleasure and with a last soft cry, Lucas gave himself to her.

He had breathed hard, holding her tightly over him until his heartbeat slowed into a gallop. Gently, reluctantly, he eased Honey down to his side, cuddling her against him. "So much for the protection I got yesterday," he had grumbled, forcing one lid open to the blinding morning light. "Sweetcakes, stop complaining..." she'd managed before he began kissing her hungrily.

Then a sharp rap on the bedroom door, followed by Jonesy's barroom bellow, cut through the sweet, lingering kiss. Lucas had cursed soundly and the day began. It ended at O'Hare Airport in Chicago with Lucas's taut expression.

Chastity straightened her round wire-rimmed glasses and discovered that the daydream of Lucas had fogged them. The jasmine tea leaves formed a pattern on the bottom of her cup and Hope was saying, "...ratings are great. The entire world is waiting for Honey and Bandit to relive their weekend...."

"Why couldn't we have just taped the thing the next day? Why did Lyle and the sponsors insist waiting this month?" Chastity asked bleakly. "Everyone else returned to the show immediately following their weekend...."

Hope glanced up from the paper's ratings. "Suspense, Chas. The camera caught the sparks between you, and the viewers loved it. If we polished you and Bandit off too fast, our ratings would flatten to pancake level. The producers say you guys are so hot together that they don't want Walkington to do the customary follow-up show with another woman."

Another woman. Lucas Walkington's well fixed body and dimples drew women like bees to flowers. The idea that Lucas was endowing his beautiful dimples and lovely, desperate lovemaking to another woman squeezed her heart painfully. If he were so impressed with her as he'd indicated after the virginity episode, he would have called. A note saying "Thanks for letting me experience your virginity" would have been nice. He'd probably forgotten the whole thing, riding his precious range with a cowgirl goddess. She discovered that she had shredded her napkin into bits.

"I don't like cliff-hangers. This thing has gone on far too long," Chastity mumbled. The twinge of uncustomary jealousy surprised her. If Lucas was passing out samples— Her nails moved on the table, aching to gently claw through that lovely curling chest hair to the dark skin beneath.

"Hey, lighten up. The sponsors sweetened the pot for you and Bandit, didn't they? Another thousand just to wait the month before the final show didn't hurt and you can pay off the Old Coot's nursing-home bill. I have to tell you, Chas. You looked supreme when you got off the plane. The studio audience went wild when they saw you kiss goodbye... although Lucas's cowboy hat hid the real thing."

"He wouldn't be interested in plain old Chastity Beauchamp," Chastity muttered and yawned. "He thinks I'm a glamour girl. If Lucas got one look at the real me, he wouldn't turn up for the show tomorrow.''

Hope dismissed Chastity's lament and went on with her last instructions, carefully itemizing Honey's beauty tips, then said, ''Chas, you've been filing too hard. You look tired. Remember to use that shadow concealer beneath your eyes tomorrow. For gosh sakes, don't carry that huge canvas tote of yours.''

''He hasn't called. He hasn't written. Gee, he sounds really eager to renew our acquaintance,'' Chastity said sarcastically. She remembered his heart pounding rapidly after their lovemaking—she hoped it survived the massive overtime when he returned to his ranch and the cowgirl goddesses.

She pictured him riding the range, supremely happy away from her, and hated him down to his boots.

The sharp, bitter emotion stunned her. She'd guarded herself since childhood against reaching out for dreams, only to be loved as desperately as Lucas had taken her.

She wanted to dump linguine over his head and down his well-stuffed jeans. She was very angry for the way he had treated Honey.

A sweet girl like Honey needed protection from dimpled cowboys with slow Oklahoma drawls.

''The guy could have been busy. Maybe his horse or his dog died or something. Who knows what can happen in greater, outer Oklahoma?''

''Women can happen,'' Chastity answered with all the dark jealousy that had been swirling in her. Lucas's kisses weren't untutored, nor was his lovemaking. She resented every woman who had tasted him. ''You forgot that Bandit might have a harem on the range.''

''Not a chance. I saw the way he looked at you. Like you were the only woman in the world. You sure are a good actress, Chas, when you try. You awed the guy down to his boots, take it from me.''

Chastity thought better of discussing how much sleep she'd been losing thinking of Lucas's lovemaking and his grim determination to leave her as quickly as he could. Clearly he wanted to place the past behind him and return home.

At least he'd never see her as plain Chastity Beauchamp. A woman who made water faucets drip. Her singular talent, according to the Old Coot, was a gift. The sexiest thing about her was Honey's pink sequin dress hanging next to her loose mix-and-match skirts and blouses.

One bitter fact remained: Lucas had not contacted Honey and Chastity hated him down to his boots.

The next day, the studio limousine took Honey, properly dressed in a cobalt-blue sheath with long sleeves and dipping bodice, to the television studio. Chastity's palms were cold and damp as she gripped Honey's small purse and pushed open the door to the studio viewing room.

Anger rode her like a nightmare, the sleepless nights wishing for Lucas in her bed swirling around her. Lucas had treated Honey horribly, giving her a taste of delight, then hoarding himself back in Oklahoma. *He deserved dimple-damage.*

Lucas stood abruptly when he saw her, his eyes darkening into a shade that matched her dress. Clad in jeans, a dress shirt and a Western leather jacket, he walked slowly toward her. He scanned her face intently while she searched her Honey vocabulary and tried to remember to lift the lazy left side of her mouth when she smiled. Her smile attempt flopped belly-up on the studio floor. "What's wrong with you?" he asked urgently, roughly, just as Lyle entered the room with a big grin.

Lucas's blue eyes darkened with anger, the lines on his face deepening throughout Lyle's happy dialogue about ratings and waiting audiences at home and in the studio. Lucas ignored Lyle's pleasantries, caught Chastity's arm and lifted her chin with the tip of his finger. "You look terrible. What's wrong?"

She frowned up at him. *He* was the problem, all six foot three of him. "I'm not happy," she stated tightly, trying to ease her arm away from his grip.

"So? I'm not either."

"You look tired," she accused, blaming him for her sleepless nights. She'd suffered Hope's beauty administrations for hours, and the footloose cowboy had the nerve to tell her she looked terrible. He could take his long, lean sexy look and—

"Hey, kids . . . kids . . . ease up," Lyle cautioned urgently, his expression of glee changed to one of distress. "We've got an audience out there at home and in the studio. They're all anxious to hear about you lovebirds—"

"Shut the hell up, Lyle," Lucas snapped as the studio intercom announced two minutes until the show began.

"Hey—" Lyle began in earnest.

"Let me handle this, Lyle," Chastity ordered. "You have no idea how ill-tempered this cowboy can be." For good measure, she thumped Lucas on the chest with her finger. No one had ever caused anger to surge through her like that dimpled, ornery cowboy. She resented that.

She frowned up at him. It was his fault that she'd become so physical, anyway. Sweet little plain Chastity would have never thought about thumping a man. Or dragging him into the studio's secluded closet and vamping him until he quivered, whispering for rescue—

"Hey, folks, show time," Hope began, then stopped as she sensed the taut scene. "Oh no, oh no. . . ."

"The studio-lounge sink faucet has just begun leaking again," another assistant said to Lyle. "Water running everywhere. Same thing happened the last time these two were here."

"Get a plumber," Lyle ordered, pale beneath his tan and makeup, while Honey and Bandit stared ominously at each other.

"You've lost weight," Lucas said in a tone resembling a growl. "Keeping too many late nights?"

Chastity sensed his jealousy, and it fueled a temper that rarely surfaced. Well, maybe when she discovered that Grace was hooked on charging goodies from the toll-free telephone numbers. Lucas had made her feel as saucy and exotic and appealing as any woman would want to be; then he zoomed off to Oklahoma and forgot her for an entire month. Logically, the deflation should have squelched his appeal, but it hadn't. "What's it to you, cowboy?" she snapped as Lyle began urging them toward the soundstage.

"Take it easy, kids," the show's host urged. "Just a few minutes on the air and you're off the hook. You won't see each other again and your nerves will settle down like *that*." He snapped his fingers, looked at Honey and Lucas, and his hopeful grin died an early death. Lyle tried again, "Remember, our audience has waited an entire month to see what's happened between you. Calm down, take a few deep breaths and everything will turn out fine."

"Like hell," Lucas muttered darkly as they walked onto the stage and his fingers locked around her waist.

No man had ever touched Chastity as though he'd never let her go, but Lucas had left her to deal with empty dreams. The thought plopped down in the pit of her stomach like lead.

"Sweetcakes, pipe down," Chastity managed in Honey's sexy tones. She wanted to strangle him, to drag him off into a corner and give him a good piece of her mind for not calling her once—not once. This ill-tempered cowboy was the reason she'd been making mistakes in filing and bookkeeping. He was the reason her appetite had slipped into the "compulsive eater" zone, though she was losing weight. He definitely was the reason she wasn't sleeping, which was possibly the reason for her sudden light-headed feeling—

Hope made a strangled noise, snatched Chastity's purse away and stepped behind a camera. Lyle patted her shoulder and whispered, "Nerves. Emotions. I've seen this happen before. The show will be great, trust me." Lyle had previously appeared on a children's show and acted professionally in disasters, swinging smoothly into his host routine.

A huge screen onstage televised the dream weekend, filled with Bandit and Honey, eating, dancing and generally enjoying each other's company. The audience cheered as gigantic, full-color Bandit swept Honey into his arms and kissed her hungrily.

Chastity watched the huge screen images of Lucas and herself deepening the kiss and closed her eyes. Her skin was clammy, her bones seemed to turn to noodles and from far away she heard Lucas's sharp exclamation, "What the—"

She had the impression of being carried in strong arms, being stretched out on a couch and having a cold washcloth placed over her forehead. Lucas's dark blue eyes searched hers, his warm hands cradling her cold ones, "Honey?"

Though his face was fuzzy, out of focus, she recognized his concern.

His voice was sweet and tender and everything she'd remembered. Because she'd frightened herself and because she knew Lucas would know what to do, she whispered, "I want to go home."

"Sure, Honey—"

"Maybe we should get the studio nurse," Lyle offered worriedly.

"The warm-up is almost done. They need to be backstage." Hope said.

"Hush up," Lucas bit out. "She's not up to games."

Chastity didn't want anyone but Lucas. She held his big hand tightly. His fingers tightened, his callused palm warm and secure around her cold hand. "Lucas, take me home."

In the next minute, she was lifted, carried, and eased into the studio limousine. Lucas cradled her against him despite her protests.

"Driver, pull over," he ordered sharply as they passed a drug store. Within moments Lucas had entered the store and returned carrying a small sack.

He snapped at the grinning chauffeur and slid next to Chastity. He tested the heat of her forehead with the back of his hand, his expression strained as the limousine began gently swaying. "Come here," he said roughly, lifting her to his lap and tucking her head against his shoulder.

"Lucas, I am fine...." she began as the auto pulled to the curb in front of her brownstone apartment building.

"Uh-huh. Sure," he agreed tightly, easing out of the deep seat, then turning to lift her out and into his arms. "You're just dandy. Peachy keen. That's why you fainted on the show."

Within minutes, Lucas placed Chastity on her ruffled quilt with an order not to move. In short time, he prepared and served a cup of steaming hot tea and crackers. He leaned against the wall to watch her.

"You're making me nervous," she murmured, noting how out of place he seemed in the feminine room. She didn't want him intruding into her privacy, didn't want him near until she could tell him what she thought about him. He'd given Honey a wonderful moment to remember, then rode off into the sunset without the slightest—

"Okay, I make you nervous," he agreed amiably, not moving while he watched her.

She blushed under the intense blue stare. "You can leave now, Lucas. You've done your good deed for the day."

His well-padded shoulder remained locked to the wall. She inhaled, fighting the distress swirling around her like icy sleet. She eased her legs toward the edge of the bed, anxious to be less vulnerable in front of his grim expression. "Lucas..."

"Get them right back up where they were," he ordered in a no-nonsense tone. "Now."

The telephone rang and Lucas snatched it from its cradle. "Yes?" The raw masculine tone held all the welcome of rawhide leather. He shot a dark look at Chastity and handed the telephone to her. "Your mother. She's ordered more jewelry and an exotic bird from a television auction...something about a credit card. The bird can recite love poems."

Lucas sat on the edge of the bed, watching with interest while Chastity tried without success to end the call. "Call you back later, Mother.... Yes, I paid last month's bill.... No, I didn't see— I'll call you back...."

He picked up a magazine she'd left near the bed, flipped to the label on the cover and studied the address closely. She frowned while her mother chattered and Lucas picked up two envelopes with her name and the same address. He studied the gold-framed pictures of Hope and other family members, then picked up the picture of Chastity and the Old Coot.

Lucas's clear blue eyes swung from her tight braids in the recent picture to Honey's curled hair. Then, standing in a lithe movement, he wandered around her bedroom until he stood facing the closet.

His long legs locked at the knee, presenting a taut backside and the impression that nothing could move him from the spot.

Chastity held her breath, aware of her mother's distress and her own as Lucas extracted the pink sequin dress. He ran one dark hand over it slowly, then scanned the other clothes with interest. He drew out cotton skirts and washable dresses, holding them high and checking the sedate hemlines. There was no question of the direction of his thoughts. Honey and Chastity were the same, yet different women.

He jerked open a bureau drawer, rummaged through the lingerie and extracted her prim panties and firm bra. He tossed her flannel granny gown on the chest, his expression thunderous. With care he opened the pair of extra glasses lying near her bed, studied the practical wire rims and looked at her, mentally placing the glasses on her nose.

"I have to go now, Mother," Chastity said firmly and replaced the receiver to the cradle as Lucas came to stand over her bed.

He placed the glasses on her nose, adjusted them to her ears and studied the effect.

The faucets in her bathroom dripped steadily away, and the clock her mother had ordered during a television auction rampage ticked loudly.

"You..." Lucas said ominously "...are Chastity Beauchamp and you could be pregnant with my baby."

Four

Chastity tried for Honey's bravado. She wished briefly for all those golden hearts she'd tossed away in Lucas's tube. He stood there in his dimples, *challenging her in her own bedroom.*

"Not a chance, sweetcakes. I'd know—" Then everything came tumbling back, the possibility dawning on her that Lucas had hit the proverbial nail on the head. She jerked the afghan lying at the foot of her bed up to her throat for protection against Lucas. He gripped it, pulling it steadily away and studying her intently from head to toe. She didn't like his predatory smile.

"You could be, Honey. Everything fits. That's why I bought one of those pregnancy kits, to see if you are." The telephone rang again, and Lucas jerked it from the cradle. "Yes?"

His jaw tensed as he listened, his blue eyes darkening with anger. "Listen, bub, you might be Chastity's brother, but where I come from you don't tell a woman to come pick you up from a bar when you've had too many afternoon drinks. Call a taxi.''

Slamming the telephone into the cradle, Lucas smiled coldly at Chastity, showing his teeth like a wolf who had just staked out his prey. He identified the caller curtly. ''Your brother. Hope is your sister and your mother is a credit-card addict. They depend on you. I'll bet you're their Little Miss Fix-it,'' he said between his teeth. ''It all fits now. When Ginger canceled, Hope had to come up with somebody fast, and you became Honey.''

''You can't take over my life like this, cowboy.'' Rigid with fury, Chastity raised slightly, only to be pinned by one big hand on her chest. The sensual tremors began immediately and Lucas's hand slid to cover her breast, his eyes darkening. She resented her body responding so blatantly to his touch, resented his intrusion into the privacy of plain, practical Chastity Beauchamp's apartment. Her refuge had been invaded by a tall, ill-tempered, maniacal cowboy without the slightest concession to her wishes. ''Go away, Lucas.''

She wanted to deal with his suggestion privately as she had always dealt with the events in her life.

''Like hell, lady.'' His words slapped the air in the frilly, delicate apartment, cutting at her. Narrowing his lids, Lucas stared at her grimly, looking as though his boots were cemented to her shaggy cream, washable rug. Her sheer floral curtains seemed to quiver.

She straightened her glasses with the tip of her finger. ''This is very rude behavior, Lucas.''

''Yep. Reckon so. You're needing someone to take care of you. Reckon that's me, so rest a bit and then we'll talk.''

Glaring at him, Chastity breathed quietly.

''Simmer down,'' he said more gently, running his hand across her cheek. There was something so comforting, so gentle in his trembling touch, that her anger suddenly melted, leaving her drained and tired. She resented the lack of energy to protect herself from Lucas's devastating touch.

"Things are complicated, Lucas."

"Sure are." His fingers played with her hair, brushing it gently.

Chastity closed her eyes, wishing she'd never allowed Hope to enter her as a Heartbeat Goddess . . . wishing she'd stayed plain old Chastity in filing and bookkeeping. She sighed wearily and wished. . . .

The faucet continued dripping and somehow the noise was comforting. She'd lived with the sound from birth, reassured that however her life had turned over, faucets still dripped when she was near.

"Go to sleep, Honey," Lucas drawled in a deep, soft voice as he removed the glasses. "We'll talk about it when you feel better. Just rest now." Then the soft afghan was replaced, tenderly tucked around her toes, and Lucas stretched out by her side, drawing her gently against him. "That's it, buttercup. Reckon we could both use some sleep."

The bathtub faucet began to drip rapidly when Lucas's big hand slid to test the weight and shape of her breasts. Chastity was too tired to think about the warm, callused palm sliding beneath her clothing to caress her softness. His thumb gently circled the tender tip and she sighed, deeply comforted by his touch. She tried to summon the strength to push him away and failed.

"Yes," he whispered sleepily, reverence in his deep drawl. "There's a difference. . . ."

Chastity awoke to the scent of coffee and the clatter of dishes in her kitchen. The clock on her bedside table blinked at her. "Seven o'clock . . . Work starts at eight!"

She whipped off the blankets and stood up to feel the cold air sheathing her body. She glanced at her singular garment, Honey's lacy, French-cut briefs, and suddenly felt woozy.

Lucas entered the room carrying a tray, scowled at her and ordered, "Get the hell back in that bed, lady."

She stared blankly at him. The sweetheart she'd bought with twenty golden hearts had changed into a raw, primitive male with raised hackles. Wearing his jeans unsnapped at the waist and nothing else, Lucas's tanned body caught the morning sun in stripes as it passed through her miniblinds. His chest hair gleamed over a tanned chest.

Chastity blinked, her woozy feeling gone. She tossed away the urge to leap on him, curling her legs around those narrow hips. She'd never had a man in her bedroom and remembered with raging fury the way Lucas had refused to leave. "Get out."

He slammed a low curse into the frothy mauve bedroom and Chastity suffered for the African violets on her window ledge. Poor things, they were used to soft encouragement and loving tones.

"Be nice," she ordered curtly, swaying slightly as the cotton rug began to rise toward her. Perhaps she needed her glasses... All those golden hearts seemed to shimmer in the "Heartbeats" tube, reminding her of the folly of falling for a deep, sexy, wistful, lonesome cowboy voice. They seemed to glow when she remembered the perfect, desperate lovemaking of her dreams that ended with Lucas's body pouring into hers.

"Get back into that bed, sweetheart," Lucas said in a too-sweet tone, as he showed his teeth in a tight smile and placed the tray on her bureau. "Please?"

Determined to hold her own, Chastity crossed her arms over her chest and hunted for her shredded dignity. "That's better, sweetcakes...I...oh, Lucas, I'm going to be ill—"

The violets were destined for another blossom-quaking round of hushed curses as Lucas swept her into his arms and carried her into the bathroom. Minutes later, he carried her back to bed, despite her protests, covered her with the warm blankets, and snapped, "Do all the faucets in this apartment drip?"

"It's a curse. My inheritance," Chastity murmured from beneath the cold washcloth covering her face. She clung to

Lucas's hard warm hand, soothed when he lifted hers to his lips and brushed kisses across the knuckles. Being cuddled and cherished in the morning was something she could grow to love, Chastity thought wearily as her stomach began to growl.

"Buttercup..." he began huskily, his mouth against her skin.

Without her glasses, the fuzzy light in his eyes resembled desire. "Lucas, I'll be late for work—"

"Honey," Lucas said firmly. "I called Charlie's. Hope gave me the number. They know you're coming in late. Someone called Sherry giggled when I told her you were sick."

Chastity jerked the cold cloth away. "Lucas, Sherry lives for gossip. She'll be spreading all sorts of stories about me. Your voice alone is enough to set her off—"

He scowled down at her and she explained quickly. "You have a slight accent—a cowboy twang—add that to deep and sexy and Sherry's mouth is off and running."

He chewed on that while he sat on the bed, watching her drink orange juice and nibble on toast. Reaching to lift a jumble of curls away from her cheek, Lucas watched Chastity's tongue forage for a crumb saturated in honey. His eyes darkened, his chest rose sharply as he inhaled. Chastity focused on that lovely contour and the way the wedge of crisp black hair narrowed down the flat, washboard muscles of his stomach. She forced her eyes to lift to his grim expression, tracing the heavy morning beard covering his jaw. "Lucas, why are you here?"

"I needed the sleep." He bit out the words. "I've missed a bit."

"That doesn't make sense, but I'm fine now. You're free to go," she said gently, formally. "There are no obligations.... You've been kind.... Thank you, Lucas."

The blue eyes blazed and his hand tightened around hers. "Just like that... thanks and get out, cowboy." Then he smiled that cold movement of lips that had nothing to do with warmth. "Think again, buttercup."

"I don't think I like the tone of that, babe," Chastity returned, recognizing the quicksilver temper that rarely lasted long when she wasn't feeling well.

"Tell you what, buttercup," Lucas said as he wrapped a curl around his dark finger and studied the contrast. "You go to work. I'll be here tonight and we can talk."

"Don't you have cows to water or chickens to feed, or—"

He smiled again and bent to kiss her parted lips. Against them he said, "I've got all the time this is going to take. You do what you have to do, and I'll do what I have to do. Seems to me like it's an even trade... for today. There are crackers in your bag. Eat them if you need to." Then he placed his open hand on her stomach and rubbed it gently. "Take care of that."

She jerked away, surprised by the easy way he touched her. "I don't want you here, Lucas. You have no right to interfere in my life, acting like a bounty hunter who's found his prey. Look, we had an experience—" His eyebrows shot up, and his head tilted arrogantly, challenging her.

Spreading her hands, Chastity took a deep breath and began again. "You're not obligated. We had a dream... a weekend away from reality. I'm having a little flu and I've always managed on my own—"

"Times have changed, buttercup. Now you have me," he said flatly.

"What did you say?" Sherry asked at four-thirty that afternoon. "Chastity, you've been mumbling all day. I think you said...'take care of what?'" Sherry's eyes widened, her lips parted and she gasped as she glanced past Chastity's shoulder, her lips parted, and she gasped.

Chastity followed Sherry's stare to the tall cowboy opening the door for two young, jean-clad women dressed in jackets with leather fringes. She removed her glasses to see better. The girls' straight glossy hair reached their waists and swung gently as they moved. They wore their jeans tucked into their boots, while Lucas wore his on the outside. The trio moved through the customers' lobby like a Western vigilante gang after bounty. Lucas's black hat almost brushed the tops of the doorframes as they entered the customer service office. Chastity clutched the thick book of overdue accounts against her for protection as Lucas and the tall girls mirroring his features stopped to ask directions.

Charlie's entire staff traced the Western trio who walked straight to the counter in front of Chastity. Lucas took off his Western hat, nodded, and said in a defensive tone, "Chastity. These are my girls, Summer and Raven. I thought they should meet you. They're ornery as the dickens, but they're mine. Same as I want you to be."

His eyes dared her to challenge him in front of his family. Her nails bit into the account book as she tried for control. It irked her that only Lucas could draw passionate emotions. He caused her to feel as though she was dancing on the line of irratic, irresponsible and definitely unprofessional behavior. He'd invaded her home and her office, presenting her with the prospect of an uncertain pregnancy, and had summoned his family posse from Oklahoma to support his takeover.

"Hello," she managed after a moment, and nodded at the girls who eyed her curiously from their six-foot heights. Six blue eyes fringed with black lashes skimmed the braids wound tightly on top of her head, then slid down her flowing blue primrose blouse and loose, long navy cotton skirt. Chastity blushed when she found Lucas's eyes darkening and touching her lips. He reached to ease a curling tendril behind her ear, then the warm fingertip slid down her hot cheek, lingered and lifted away reluctantly. Hunger, unshielded, tangled and heated the air between them for a moment before Lucas took the heavy book away from her. He placed it firmly on the counter with a look that dared her to pick it up. "Too heavy," he said firmly, placing her glasses on her nose. "Don't lift anything that weighs over five pounds from now on."

Chastity wanted to scream, refusing to adjust the tilted angle of the glasses. Lucas defined rules, intruded and acted as if he had the right to do so. She resented that deeply. While she was thinking about a proper retort, Lucas's dimples played in his cheeks as though he was smothering a pleased grin.

"Nice meeting you, ma'am," Raven said quietly, shooting an impish expression up at her father, while Summer worked to smother the brilliant smile tugging at her lips.

"It's nice to meet you." Chastity touched her braids self-consciously as the girls continued to inspect her, clearly in awe. "I'm afraid 'Heartbeats' wanted me to look..."

She glanced at Lucas. He hadn't said a word about being disappointed. He knew that Honey was a fabricated fluff designed for a camera, *and he hadn't said a word.* The quick flush ran up her cheeks and heated her throat. The poor guy must be laden with guilt, accepting his punishment on those broad shoulders. There wasn't a thing luscious or desirable about her. Then Lucas's blue eyes pinned the heavy pulse at the base of her throat.

His finger rested on it lightly and his mouth tightened. "The word is 'sexy.'"

His expression said he wanted to carry her away that moment. Sherry gasped somewhere in the outer stratosphere and another clerk dropped a stack of papers.

Chastity's lips parted with a thought she couldn't think as Lucas's finger rose to caress her chin. They were alone then, wrapped in something she didn't understand.

Summer elbowed Lucas and his finger lingered, then moved away as if he didn't want to stop touching her. "She's prettier than on television."

Chastity glanced at her sharply, but the girl wasn't teasing, her expression open as her outdoor heritage. "I... I... they lightened my hair... then the makeup and training..."

Lucas glanced impatiently at the clock. "You get off at five. We'll wait in the lobby. I cooked supper while I waited for the girls' plane. They just got in." Then he smiled warmly at Sherry, who was gripping the counter tightly, her eyes jerking between the four of them. "Don't mind us. I'm Honey's—Ms. Beauchamp's intended husband and these are my girls."

Then he reached, cupped Chastity's jaw in his warm, rough palms and drew her mouth to his for a lingering kiss that left her dazed.

Sherry's soft whoosh of air exploded as Lucas shot a hot, meaningful stare at Chastity. He and the girls left to wait in the customer's lobby. Through the windows, Chastity finished her work beneath the girls' stealthy stares.

Later, in the sanctity of her bedroom, Chastity exploded. "Lucas, explain yourself. You walked into Charlie's, started the gossip mill churning, and—"

"Have you taken that test yet?" he demanded, crossing his arms over his chest.

Definitely a challenging male, Lucas was just short of breaking her well-known patience. "No, I haven't had time, and the directions say it's a morning test—"

"You make time in the morning, lady, and we'll take it from there...the four of us, together. If you're pregnant—"

"Lucas!" Her impatient scream drew giggles from the living room.

He jerked open the door and ordered, "Summer. Raven. That's enough. Set the table. We'll be out in a few minutes."

"Daddy, you be nice to her," one girl warned while the other giggled.

Lucas shut the door. "Sassy-mouthed, ornery—" Then he looked at the smile Chastity tried to hide. His expression lit and warmed and suddenly he flashed that devastating all-male grin and drawled sexily, "Come here, you."

Before she could resist, Lucas's kiss melted and heated, filled with hunger and desire and promises. When it was done, she leaned limply against Lucas's hard thighs, his heart racing beneath her hot cheek. Sometime during the tropical storm, the lightning crashing and the hunger racing, she'd locked her hands into his tooled Western belt. Now her fingers refused to leave their mooring. Her glasses were steamed and slanted across her nose. She feared the heated kiss had bent the wire rims.

Poor unsexy Chastity Beauchamp shivered in confusion, while Honey wanted to take Lucas down to the creamy shag rug.

"The way I see it," he said unevenly, his hands trembling as he cuddled her against him, "is this—one step at a time. Take the test, then we'll see what happens."

He bent to kiss the tip of her nose, his eyes very blue behind the steam covering her lenses. "If you don't, buttercup, reckon the girls and I can camp here until I know otherwise." Then he patted her bottom, ran his palm across her tummy and gave her a look that said he wished they were alone.

The next morning, Chastity shivered behind her bedroom door, breathed deep and searched for courage. "Ah . . . Lucas, could you come in here?" she asked.

The girls smothered giggles when their father halted his long-legged stride across the room to glare at them. "Hush up, tidbits," he ordered gently, his eyes locked on Chastity's face.

Chastity sat on the bed, rereading the kit's instructions, and tried to ignore Lucas's clean, soapy scent. She hadn't slept all night, aching for him to hold her.

This morning her living room couch and floor were filled with Walkingtons; the girls slept deeply, but Lucas's sleepy gaze had stopped her on her way to the kitchen. "Mornin', buttercup," he'd whispered, and the drawl echoed with needs that started her heart racing and her stomach fluttering.

Now he eased onto the bed, placed his arm around her and waited. She liked the quiet way he held her cold hand on his thigh. "We're in trouble, according to this," she whispered after a moment, her hands trembling and cold.

How could she have conceived so soon?

"No, we're not, Honey. Everything is just fine." He tipped her chin up with the tip of his finger and she looked into his clear blue eyes. "I want this baby and I want you."

"But, Lucas, we're so different—" Images of bills, her mother's credit-card gambits, Hope's job, Brent's troubled affairs and the problems of assorted relatives swirled through her head.

"Honey, we'll take it one step at a time." Then he removed her glasses and kissed her and savoring the sweet, tender taste, Chastity kissed him back.

Then she was lying on her back and Lucas was nuzzling her neck gently. She touched his upper arms lightly, pressing the hard, tense muscles. Running her palm behind his neck, she smoothed the taut power with a caress and Lucas stilled, letting her wander through her thoughts.

She stroked his black waves, waiting for his breath to warm her throat. Lucas felt like eternity. As though he would always be there, solid and close to her.

Lucas Walkington, the babe, the sweetcakes, the one-hundred-percent-certified male, wanted her. He trembled then, the vulnerable movement endearing him to her. Chastity closed her eyes sleepily, warmed by his heat, and stroked his back lightly.

She wanted this man desperately, greedily. She wanted whatever time she could have to hold him just like this. She'd waited for a special man, waited for a family of her own, and nothing could stop her from taking the risk. "Yes," she whispered.

He relaxed slightly against her as if relieved; the press of his chest against her surprised her and she realized that he had been holding his breath. "Yes," she said again, more firmly. "Let's go for it, babe."

Then she yawned, dropping into the sleep that had been closing gently on her.

"One step at a time," Chastity repeated two days later as the big Chevrolet Suburban that Lucas had rented eased out of Chicago. Dawn fought its way through her plants and boxes filling the spacious interior. In the aftermath of Lucas's vulnerability, she realized one poignant fact: she had as much resistance to him as she did to double-Dutch, maraschino topped, triple-fudge cake with walnuts.

She'd grabbed Lucas like a brass ring for a weekend in paradise and now her entire life was out of control. He was a disaster as a gentleman, looping his fingers around her wrist as though he was afraid she would run away at any moment.

He moved quickly, with deadly intent tinged with desperation.

Within the space of a day, Lucas had plopped his daughters on a return trip to Oklahoma and packed her things. When she returned home that evening after giving her notice, he had cooked dinner, laundered and purchased assorted prenatal-care books. Her relatives began appearing and Lucas graciously served them his home-style chili and jalapeño corn bread. He planted gentle, but distinct hints about Chastity needing rest and care, which caused her to want to scream. When her mother protested and cried, Lucas handed her his freshly ironed handkerchief. "I'll take good care of her, ma'am. We're getting married just as soon as possible. But Chastity won't have time to baby-sit your credit-card situation. Reckon you'll have to bite the bullet."

With that he had lifted the back of Gracie's hand and kissed it, totally captivating her. The dimples flashed full force. "It's easy to see that you're Chastity's mother. She's got your beauty and intelligence. Then there's the sweetness, too. You must have been very young when you became a mother. I hope our baby has those same lovely green eyes. Like new spring grass.''

Grace had flushed and giggled. She patted her wedge of curly hair and asked Lucas about his ranch. Mildly disappointed when he explained the simple, budget life-style in spacious Oklahoma, Grace was quickly swept under Lucas's charm, which Chastity noted he dragged out when needed. Grace thought it was "cute" and almost swooned with romantic delight when he swept up Chastity, who had been dozing on and off, and carried her into the bedroom.

One startling thought nagged Chastity. Lucas could be devastating, charming when he wanted, or ornery and stubborn when it suited him.

Why was she sitting in a Suburban driven by a cowboy, headed for outer Oklahoma?

She had wanted to protest his takeover, but the incredible fatigue draining her body prevented a mutiny. She dozed through Lucas's cleaning and packing and whirlwind arrangements with Hope's help. Her sister arranged for a temporary secretary to shoulder the remainder of her week's notice. Charlie loved the mini-ad on "Heartbeats," another trade-off that Hope had arranged. In the end, Chastity slept, tried not to focus on her growing confusion and wondered who was doing what to package her as Lucas's bride-to-be. Everyone seemed immensely happy for her. If she could wake up fully, she would toss him out on his wellshaped rear.

His game plan lacked a few finer points like asking her opinion.

Lucas never mentioned love or commitment or whispered little nothings.

She did not want Lucas to feel obligated to sweep her off her feet, much less marry her.

Once she got control of her tired, drained and sleeping self, she would regain her senses. She'd stepped out for a wonderful, memorable weekend, something to tuck away for her old age and suddenly Lucas was grimly—yes, grimly—determined to pirate her to Oklahoma without a word of love or romance.

Chastity frowned at an encroaching vine of wandering Jew that bobbed on her shoulder. She replaced it carefully. She was a practical woman who knew that love and romance belonged in fairy tales. Some deep, dark, secret part of her must have been inherited from her romantic mother. The whole adventure was doomed for disaster.

Once she awoke fully, she'd weigh the situation and come to a sensible conclusion.

"Bite the bullet," Chastity repeated darkly as Lucas sipped his morning coffee, while deftly steering the Suburban onto an interstate highway. "You evidently called Hope and she maneuvered the rest of the family into thinking this Oklahoma thing was best for everybody... including the show's ratings."

"Something like that." Lucas nodded, watching traffic closely. His profile resembled that of an intent wagon train master plotting his course on the prairie. He'd pulled out the charm and buttered up every woman who could lessen his chances to snatch her away. Brent had tasted a bitter lash of male disdain and Chastity wasn't certain what else, but after a private conversation with Lucas, her brother had shown signs of terror. Now Lucas sat beside her, pirating her away to Oklahoma. Her glasses were safely tucked in his shirt pocket.

"Magic between Heartbeat Goddess and Bandit turns to love, is that right?"

"Yep. She bought it. We won't have to turn up on the show again. Some little clause about relatives not participating—"

"You used blackmail?" The high-pitched squeak twirled around a huge elephant leaf plant and the boxes, and dropped between them.

Chastity stared at him through the shadows of the cab's interior. A leaf on her lemon tree quivered. "I have no idea who you really are—as a person. Or why I'm sitting here beside you. Or Oklahoma ranching. Oh, Lucas, *why am I sitting here?*" she asked desperately. "You don't have to do any of this. Why are we here?"

He slowly placed his cup in the dash holder, reached out an arm and scooped her against him. "Because we've made a baby. Because I want to take care of you. Because if I left you in that bleeding heart hornet's nest, you might get sick."

"I feel," she said carefully, wearily, "like I am being drafted."

"That's right, buttercup. The only thing you have to do on my ranch is care for yourself. You'll have plenty of fresh air on the ranch and good care. We live simple and I want you to know there's not much excitement or money out on the ranch." He stated the last part slowly, his expression hard, as though it had cost him a measure of pride. "I work away when I can, picking up odd jobs. There's not much employment around Chip."

Chastity thought of spending every waking moment near Lucas. Oklahoma looked marvelous.

He was acting gallantly, paying his obligation to care for her, even plunging into marriage because of a dream weekend. The result would be disastrous. The odds for a successful venture were less than okay, closer to low.

"This is a big mistake," she managed sleepily from Lucas's safe, broad shoulder, afraid that her brief moment of ecstasy could be swept away forever. "I've lived in the city all my life. I quit eating beef when I realized it came from cows with those pretty brown eyes. Maybe I'm not pregnant. We should have waited for a doctor—"

She forced inches between them and blinked up at him, refusing to reach into his pocket for her glasses. "Oh, Lucas, you told Mother that we were getting married. If you want to tell your friends that we are, I won't mind. Or that we're not and I'm a cousin or something. Or you could just put me back on a bus."

She wanted her safe, frilly bedroom, her predictable job at Charlie's, and the never-ending disasters of her family. She was comfortable in her life-style; it suited her to be in control of her emotions. She barely recognized greed, but it was there every time she thought about Lucas. Deep, challenging anger was a new emotion she'd discovered since meeting him.

Living with Lucas would be a disaster. The whole event was a fiasco from top to bottom.

She frowned. *Something was definitely wrong. Lucas was acting out of his sense of honor and obligation. She didn't want a life built on his sacrifice.*

Lucas tugged her back gently to his shoulder and stroked her hair, which helped her growing headache. "It's not likely a mistake, Honey. I've thought about it since I saw you. Making love with you was a natural thing to do. Just like making a baby. I sensed it then, like part of me became yours, like cherishing."

When he said things like that, her skidding resistance rolled over into a pleasant "okay."

"I'm nothing like Honey, you know. I'm just plain old Chastity Beauchamp," she whispered sleepily against a tanned throat that she couldn't resist kissing. The strong pulse running beneath his warm skin felt like an eternity of sunshine and rainbows. "I'm a modern woman. I can have and raise a baby alone."

"Not likely. Not my baby, anyway, and there's no other yahoo in the picture, the way I see it," Lucas stated flatly as she slid into the safety of sleep.

Five

Lucas tightened his hand on the steering wheel and cuddled Chastity's soft body nearer his. He'd calf-roped her into moving to Oklahoma, hadn't given her time for second thoughts. He'd reached out and grabbed what he wanted desperately, disregarding the consequences. He wasn't a boy now, polishing his honor and owning up to spending too many nights experimenting in a back seat. He knew he was acting instinctively, grabbing with both fists what he wanted and dragging Chastity into his life. She was the kind of woman to expect love—

Love. Lucas turned the word around, studying the facets. His throat tightened against the thought. At thirty-eight he wasn't likely to experience that kid's disease. He wouldn't let himself get ripped up a second time. More likely he'd found a woman who soothed the lonely ache within him. Marriages and affairs were based on less than love; people worked on relationships, caring for one another.

He wouldn't ask Chastity to take on his problems, he wanted to keep her tucked away, safe and rested.

That didn't explain the savage anger that erupted when he discovered Chastity's role in the family. She was somewhere between a doormat, a banker, a psychiatrist and a mother.

He couldn't desert her in that swamp of users. He wanted to cherish and cuddle and protect her.

Lucas scowled at a young couple kissing in the front seat of a passing pickup. He'd played the love game as a youngster. This go-round wasn't clear yet, but he intended to keep Chastity tucked beside him until the dust settled.

He checked her seat belt, adjusted the angle of her legs against his and settled down to drive the long interstate highway with his hand on her thigh. Traveling down the interstate, taking his woman to his home, was right and inevitable, filling him with a quiet joy. Chastity sighed softly against his skin and the hair on the back of his neck rose immediately. She was sweet and soft, and if ever he'd known a woman to be a good thing—Chastity was that woman. He hadn't hesitated to snatch her from that grasping family mob. The thought of his baby in the midst of that bloodsucking crew—his knuckles turned white on the steering wheel.

Chastity slept beside him, her head resting on a pillow now and Lucas traced the way the spring sun entered the window to glisten in the single braid that lay over her chest. Suddenly Lucas found his finger stroking the thick braid, catching its warmth and fragrance. He ran his thumb across the loose tip, allowing the curls to lick and twine around his hand.

He bore the scars of heartbreak and didn't want to need Chastity desperately, achingly.

Alesha had fascinated him in the wild hunger of youth. Drawn him into a world that shimmered and heated, then ripped him apart as a man. He'd fought to match her needs, the demands of her wealthy family, and lost himself for a time in a social whirl that almost sucked him into an empty abyss. In the end, she agreed to have the twins, then snatched them from his "ugly, broken-down cattle farm" and tucked them into a mansion for three years.

A big semitrailer passed Lucas and the Suburban lurched in the wind's force. Lucas found Chastity's soft hand, drew it to his thigh, and laced his fingers with hers. He'd found her by mistake and pounced with the deadly intent of keeping her near him.

He'd heard how some women slept often during the first weeks of their pregnancy and suspected that Chastity's dozing was that symptom. He wasn't above using her weakness to get her back to his ranch. He was walking on eggs, realizing that she could wake fully at any minute and change her mind. The desperation racing in Lucas frightened him.

He should know better; should know that things were better left alone.

Damn. He wanted her with him. Feared that at any moment he'd lose her.

The whole thing was headed for a cow pile. She'd take one look at his ranch, the house and the way he worked at any job possible to pay bills, then she'd hightail it back to Chicago. The whole thing could fall apart at any minute.

Just past Springfield, Missouri, Chastity grumbled as he carried her into the motel room. When he slipped off her shoes, she roused sleepily and swatted his hands. She sighed as he stripped her down to her panties and tugged his T-shirt over her head. Within minutes, Lucas smiled in the dark as Chastity's soft thigh eased gently across his thigh to rest within his legs. Her arm flung across his chest and she murmured "Mmm" with pleasure as she stroked the hair on his chest. In the next sleepless hour, Lucas tensed each time she moved, nestling closer.

Nothing but soft cotton separated them as Chastity eased over him entirely and settled down to sleep comfortably. Lucas couldn't force himself to place her aside, couldn't stop his body from responding to the soft heat of hers. Within seconds, she tensed, inhaled sharply and pushed her hands against the pillow they shared. He kept his lids closed, feigning sleep, and enjoyed the moment. Confused, she blinked, and eased away from Lucas. He couldn't resist grabbing her wrist, reluctantly releasing her. "Bed hog," he accused, wanting to draw her beneath him—

"Oh, I'm so sorry. I'm...I need the bathroom." She searched desperately for the bathroom, then ran to it, presenting Lucas with the tantalizing view of her rounded bottom where her panties had inched higher.

Placing his hands behind his head, he waited and enjoyed the sound of her bathing. Within a half hour, she called gently, "Ah...Lucas?"

He fought the grin teasing his mouth and remained quiet. She reminded him of a cuddly soft little bunny rabbit, curiously approaching something that fascinated her. After several moments, she whispered, "Lucas? Are you awake?"

She opened the bathroom door slightly and a wedge of light sliced across him. He traced her progress to the bed from beneath his lashes. Draped in the long-sleeve shirt he had discarded earlier, Chastity eased onto the other bed. She sat with crossed legs and clutching a pillow to her chest. The dim light tangled in her loose hair, creating a halo as she studied him and brushed her hair. "What am I doing?" she muttered quietly. "Of course he's delectable. But what am I doing?" After a few more angry strokes, she whispered, "This is all Hope's fault."

"Delectable says get into bed," Lucas said quietly and watched her expressions range from surprise to chagrin.

"You're awake, you jerk!" She launched the pillow at him and Lucas tossed it back gently. "You undressed me!"

"Lighten up, buttercup, I need my beauty sleep. First you roll all over me, trying to seduce me in my sleep, and then you mutter and keep me awake. Get into bed." He anticipated her next move with delight.

"You are a strange man, Lucas Walkington," she said in a hushed, wary tone. "Thank you for your thoughtfulness—setting out my traveling case, but *I am not a buttercup,*" she added in a dignified and quiet explosion.

Lucas turned on his side, studying her in the darkness. There were long legs and a frothy mist of hair, the nudge of soft curves beneath his shirt. She looked and smelled sweet. "Buttercup," he said firmly, enjoying the way she cornered her rising temper and pressed her lips together. He felt like a boy with his first girl, tormenting her for the sheer pleasure of getting her attention.

"My hair is not blond, Lucas. It's light, mouse-brown. Buttercup must be some sort of odd family name," she returned haughtily, easing into the empty bed.

A truck soared by on the highway outside, and Chastity said quietly, "I don't like the idea of you acting out of some ancient idea of honor, Lucas. You are not obligated to do any of this."

"A man does what he has to do," he returned, his body rigid. At any moment, she'd say that she was leaving him—

"What do you have to do, Lucas?" she asked in a breath of a whisper.

"Keep you," he said truthfully, realizing that the wrong word, the wrong tone could send her running away from him.

"Why?" The word trembled in the shadows, scurrying around his heart.

"I want you with me," he answered, his stomach hurting with pain.

He waited for her to reply and when she didn't, he closed his lids, waiting. The minutes stretched into a half hour and he realized that she slept. Lucas settled down to sleep with the thought that at least his shirt was snuggled up to her. A half hour later, he eased out of bed, scooped her up gently and deposited her into his bed. Before he slept fully, Lucas adjusted Chastity into his arms, keeping her close, and nuzzled her fragrant, damp hair. She was just what he needed to warm the ache that had been with him for an eternity.

At a truck-stop café near their motel, Chastity replaced the glass of orange juice firmly on the booth's table. Lucas had devoured three pancakes with butter and syrup, six slices of bacon, three eggs and an entire plate of hash brown potatoes. He sipped coffee, oblivious to the waitress in the tight uniform who sidled by their booth with lingering, hungry looks.

"I think," Chastity said calmly despite the raging anger that had brewed in her since they'd walked into the café and Lucas had drawn women's hungry eyes, "that this farce has gone too far." She adjusted her glasses primly. "I think we should call this whole thing off and return to our respective corners. For some unknown reason, you have a disastrous effect on me. We couldn't possibly live together. I am a calm, reasonable woman, and your tendencies to order me about are grating."

That statement drew a masculine brow upward. "We're not suited to each other," she said, foraging for strength that dissolved the moment Lucas touched her. She shivered slightly, trying to place the morning's embarrassment behind her. She had awakened sprawled over Lucas's aroused body. He'd been gruff and abrupt when he awoke, piling her into the Suburban without a drop of the devastating charm he'd spread for her mother. "I don't like..." she began carefully as he scowled at her.

In her lifetime, she'd rarely stood her ground for her own interests. The insight rustled through her, raising an anger that never surfaced when she was plain Chastity. Lucas's ability to unbalance her had to be stopped. "I really don't like being hustled into a temporary arrangement we probably will regret. You feel obligated to do your duty, and while that's marvelous, it's really not practical. I've never been a burden to anyone, and I don't want to start now. We can't ruin our lives for a moment when we..."

Her fingers spread out and she noticed with distress that they were shaking. If Lucas didn't stop shooting her those blue-eyed passionate looks—*Lucas was very bad for her control. She had never met a man who could make her feel so violent, so feminine, so utterly bothered.*

He lounged back in his seat, shot a devastating thank-you grin at the waitress who had just filled his cup, and looked at Chastity with dark blue eyes. Her resolve to grasp control of her life since meeting Lucas began slipping. She spread her hand out on the table's cool surface and hoped that her morning nausea would not resurface. "Look, there might not be a baby. This whole thing is a mistake. I'm not anything near a Heartbeats Goddess. You won't be happy. You'll hate me . . . *and I'm so sleepy I can't think,*" she finished in a soft plea. "Lucas, this arrangement is not logical. Here we are . . . somewhere . . ." She looked desperately for reality and it scurried out into the Missouri sunshine.

Lucas let her sit there in the booth and sink in oozing, cold fear. She could have killed him for that. He was nothing like the gallant who kissed her mother's hand and charmed everyone she knew in Chicago. The sun glittered on the tips of his blue-black lashes and Chastity fought touching them. The thought that he was so beautifully touchable angered her. Beneath that dark skin, jutting cheekbones and the lurking dimples that charmed feminine hearts at will, was a dark moody temper, a possessive streak, a chauvinistic steel will and a man who kidnapped her out of Chicago's safety. Chastity took a deep breath, tried to ignore the way those blue eyes jerked immediately to her sensitive chest, and rummaged for all the drama she had learned from Old Coot. *Play it to top, wring it for every drop.* "I am not going to let this happen. You are not ruining your life, nor mine, for some antiquated masculine, chauvinistic idea of male honor. Put me on a bus for Chicago."

Lucas's smoky blue eyes locked with hers, and his fingers gripped her wrist. "Like hell, lady."

Her control slipped slightly. "You are not lassoing a cow, Lucas—"

"Heifer," he corrected with a sexy drawl. "Top grade."

Chastity tossed her head, ignoring the wispy tendrils that refused to stay confined in her braid. "Whatever brand of cattle you want to name is fine. The point is, you can be mean and ornery. Quite unlike any man I want to live with, let alone…" Reaching for an expression, Chastity sailed out a hand and found her other wrist snagged firmly. She realized that her lenses had distorted the distance and she had almost toppled over a pitcher of syrup. "This is just too fast—"

"You're cute in the morning," he drawled while she tried to find a dram of sanity from the moment she posed as Honey.

"Cute?" Chastity shook her head, dazed. She'd been labeled "well-groomed," "neat and dressed sedately," but no one had ever referred to her as anything but plain Chastity Beauchamp.

"If the baby is a boy, we could name him 'Beau' for Beauchamp. That way your family name would be carried on, too." Then Lucas drew her palms to his mouth and licked each center gently. While something inside her turned to sunlight, butterflies and spring rain, Lucas suckled her fingertips. "Your eyes just turned to evening meadow green, buttercup. There are gold flecks around the black, and that's filled with me," he whispered huskily. "Sure takes the years out of this old man."

Poised to pour more coffee, the waitress gasped, and Lucas hauled out two adorable dimples, catching Chastity in midbreath. "We'll do fine," he said.

Scrimmaging for control, Chastity gripped his hands tightly. "Lucas, I haven't the foggiest about farm life," she managed desperately. "Clearly this is a mistake. I'm not ready to make this commitment. I've promised myself a marriage based on love, not convenience. Please put me on a bus. We'll correspond if you like."

"I'll take you back to Chicago and that bunch of free-loaders you call family," he said, playing with the tip of her fat braid, watching the light turn it to gold. "But I'm staying wherever you are until a doctor says that you're pregnant—and you are, buttercup. I know it in my bones. I knew when I gave you my baby. The choice is up to you. We can turn around right now—"

"You have a ranch, responsibilities and the girls." She couldn't force herself to ask if he felt one tiny, itty bitty bit of love for her, if he could possibly dredge up the enthusiasm to perhaps slip a little romance into the adventure. Of course she wasn't a romantic woman; she was practical and faucets dripped when she was near. Maybe he thought that once back in Oklahoma, he could transform her into Honey forever.... Her stomach contracted and she yawned, filled with a sense of disaster.

Lucas was pure common sense. "Summer and Raven wouldn't like it if I came home empty-handed. They're pretty happy to have another female to bear the burden of an old hermit daddy."

"Old hermit daddy," she repeated blankly, trying to fit the description to Lucas's vibrant, sexy image.

"Buttercup, don't leave me to face those monsters alone," he cajoled in that deep, sexy Oklahoma twang. "They're mean, ornery and have half the boys in Oklahoma stirred up."

He tugged her braid, ran a fingertip slowly across her mouth and said, "I'm just a rangy old cowboy looking for a little warmth in his remaining years. Buttercup, I purely want what we've got together and maybe with God's blessings, what we've made together." The dimples deepened and Chastity fought not to touch them. Lucas removed her glasses and tucked them in his pocket with the air of a man successfully completing a mission.

By the time she recovered, she was tucked safely in the Suburban and too drowsy to rally a good mutiny. She dropped off to sleep with Lucas holding her hand and whistling "Home on the Range."

Chastity felt like a princess scooped away by a dashing prince. The wrinkle in the fairy tale was Lucas's desperate sense of old-fashioned obligation and the fact that he could be in love with Honey, not herself.

She dozed, awaking just as he slid into the driver's seat after filling the gasoline tank. Shaking her head slightly, Chastity spoke the thought that had been worrying her for miles. "Lucas, don't expect...we're not going to...ah, you know...."

Apparently Lucas had been circling the same thought. He nibbled on her lips. "Wouldn't think of doing anything before you asked me, buttercup. You have my word on it. You let me know when you think the time is right. To make sure I don't jump the gun before you're ready, you're going to ask."

Hours later, Chastity awoke slightly as Lucas eased her into his arms. The crisp night air swirled around him, cows mooed and two girls whispered in hushed excitement. "Put me down," she ordered, thrashing her way free of the soft blanket in which he had wrapped her. She blew a row of curling tendrils from her forehead. "You've got to stop carrying me everywhere."

"Buttercup, we're home," Lucas stated with deep pride, placing her on the linoleum floor of his kitchen.

A dog yelped frantically, bobbing around Lucas's long, jean-clad legs. When he bent to rub the poodle's white, furry head, the dog licked happily at his hand. "That's Wayne," Lucas said, tossing his hat to the table. He adjusted her glasses and grinned.

Chastity blinked, looking up at the two teenage girls who stood in disreputable sweatpants and Lucas's old shirts. He tucked her against him, one hand resting lightly on her hip as he faced the twins. "Have you girls stirred up any trouble since we parted?"

"No, Daddy," they chorused innocently, studying Chastity closely. She blushed under their intent blue eyes.

"Did Mrs. Biddlecomb call?"

"Yes, Daddy. She's been over every day checking on us," Raven said with a defensive edge to her voice. "I told her we could manage for these few days, but she insisted on coming anyway. Her and that snoopy sister of hers. They want to meet Honey."

When Raven floundered, Lucas glanced quickly at Chastity, then said, "My future wife, that's what she is. We'll arrange it tomorrow."

"Lucas . . ." Chastity pressed her hand against her stomach, which had been growling slightly. She didn't want to upset his children by expressing her doubts. Nor mentioning the way he hadn't stopped to ask her opinion along the way. She immediately sympathized with the girls, whose expressions said they thought the whole adventure was romantic.

Summer reached to touch her hand, blushed and whispered reverently, "Oh, gosh, Daddy. This is so exciting. We're going to have our own little baby."

Looking up, Chastity was amazed to see Lucas blush beneath his deep tan. "Yep. If things work out."

Both girls giggled and leaped on him, the impact taking him back and down to the couch. Lucas struggled amid a web of long limbs and then he chuckled. The brief, deep sound enchanted Chastity and she listened for another, which did not come. Amazingly the trio rolled to the floor without interrupting the giggles. The girls scrambled to their feet, and Lucas lay looking up at Chastity. He looked rumpled and adorable, his shirt opened to expose his stomach, his hair tousled. Wayne managed to scoot under his hand for petting. Lucas's dimples deepened amid dark stubble and he said unevenly, "Welcome home, buttercup."

Both girls pivoted toward her, their eyes widening. "Buttercup? Daddy calls you 'buttercup'?" they chorused, bending to take Lucas's boots and drag him a short distance.

"Lay off," he said, grinning sleepily and looking marvelously all-male. "Watch your manners. She's half-ready to run away now. If you two start acting like savages, she might take off."

Summer and Raven straightened slowly and frowned at Chastity. "You wouldn't take our baby away, would you?" Raven asked cautiously. She glanced down at her father, who lay there watching the females with interest, his hands behind his head. "Get up and behave, Dad. Your horseplay might scare her away."

Her sister glanced from Lucas to Chastity with interest. "Dad, you just laughed for the first time in years," she noted in a startled tone as the kitchen sink began dripping steadily.

Lucas rose slowly to his full height and tugged Chastity's braid. "Go lay down. The girls and I will bring in your things. We'll take the car back to the rental place first thing in the morning." When Chastity glanced at the cozy living room and the doors leading from it, Lucas nodded toward a bedroom. "That's my room. We've got one bathroom."

When she hesitated, determined to salvage a tiny dram of her pride, he looked at the girls and nodded toward the Suburban. "Git."

Chastity swallowed uncertainly as he glanced at the television set. The girls had been replaying tapes of Bandit and Honey, school books and a bowl of popcorn lay on the floor. On-screen Honey slid into the tall cowboy's path, demanding her kiss. Her eyes were green and hungry, her mouth glossy and parted. Standing behind her, Lucas wrapped Chastity in his arms and swayed gently. He fitted his chin on top of her head and watched Honey's hungry expression. "We're home now, buttercup," he whispered gently. "I haven't got much to offer you but two ornery daughters, and clean air and sunshine. We'll take care of you."

Chastity fought fatigue and the urge to punch his dimples. "Lucas, I'm used to taking care of myself. I take care of other people."

His big hand covered her stomach and he soothed it as he swayed her in his arms. She could have stayed like that all night, warm and cherished, wrapped in Lucas. "We'll manage, at least until we know about the baby. We'll work it out after that. I won't hold you if you want to go, buttercup...."

The ache in his voice wound around her heart and Chastity closed her eyes. Lucas rocked her gently, his body tense behind her, his hand firmly on her stomach. "This is wrong—"

"Can't be. Nothing can be wrong that feels this right," he said simply as he kissed her temple.

"Lucas," she began again, staring at the open bedroom door, which symbolized her life with him. Somewhere in greater Chicago, her mother, Brent and Hope needed her care. The faucet dripped in her apartment bathroom without anyone to scowl at it. "I don't know."

"Hush up, buttercup," he whispered unevenly. "Bed down in my room for tonight and I'll take the couch. We'll get married in the morning, when we return the car. After that, reckon we'll take it a step at a time."

"Lucas, marriage is a little drastic for the situation. Marriage for convenience is worthy in some cases, but not necessary with me. Marriages are for love and commitment—"

"I'm committed, buttercup," Lucas stated tightly. "Love is a dream. We can make things work."

"I am so tired," she whispered drowsily. Any minute Lucas would wake up and accuse her of entrapment. Of presenting a luscious dream girl as bait, then sticking him with a woman with short, practical fingernails.

"Lady..." Lucas lifted her gently into his arms and carried her into the dark bedroom. "Get this straight. You worry too much. That's what I'm for, to worry and to lean on. You take it easy from now on.''

''If I weren't so tired, I'd argue,'' she returned with a yawn. ''This won't work. Will you stop carrying me?''

His arms tightened and she realized that no one had cuddled her for an eternity. In the morning she'd wake up, find reality and save them both from disaster, but just now she nestled against him.

The room smelled like Lucas, safe and warm and dark. The furniture was sturdy, made from oak that would last like steel. There was a scarred desk with boxes of papers stacked beneath it. Photographs of his daughters and old brown-tinted pictures studded the tan plaster walls. Lucas held her as he walked to the wall, nodding to a framed picture of the twins as babies. ''Twins,'' he said slowly, watching her expression in the shadows.

''They're beautiful,'' she said, admiring the fat cheeks and masses of black hair.

He held her a moment longer, as if he wanted to say something more, then decided against it. Gently Lucas placed her on her feet. He swallowed, ran his hand over her cheek and hair, and bent to kiss her. ''You rest, buttercup. The girls and I will take care of you.''

Too weary to debate his orders, Chastity waited until the door closed, then sat slowly. ''Here I am in Oklahoma. Why?'' Then she looked at the comfortable, clean white pillows amid the huge wood-frame bed and decided all decisions could wait until the morning.

Morning lurched at her in blinding sunlight, and beyond the bedroom door, a hushed Walkington argument was brewing. ''Git,'' Lucas said in the same no-nonsense tone as he had used the previous night.

''We want to stay home from school today, Daddy. Chastity needs help, and you're grouchy and tired....''

Chastity waited for traffic sounds to begin, for the scurry of people going to work passing her apartment doorway.

She hugged the warmth of the old bed, stretching beneath the weight of the quilt, which smelled like wind and sunshine.

A dove cooed beyond the window and the smell of fresh coffee slid through the wedge of sunlight crossing to the bed. She felt thrillingly awake and alive, stretching again and wiggling her toes.

"You're going to school today," Lucas said more firmly over the clatter of dishes.

"I've never been in a wedding. Daddy, it's early yet. No one knows that this is a shotgun wedding—"

"Hush," Lucas snapped.

"I want to show her my new calf," Raven said. "Rosebud is pretty."

Wayne barked wildly and somewhere in Chicago a taxi cab driver cursed and honked at blocked traffic.

The Oklahoma dove cooed again and Chastity whispered, "Shotgun wedding."

Lucas's flannel robe lay across the foot of the bed as a reminder of his possession.

She eased to her elbows and closed her eyes. "Heartbeat Goddess... Charlie's bookkeeper... the bride in an Oklahoma shotgun wedding..."

Lucas had kept her moving, carrying her where he wanted her. Her hands closed into fists. He'd picked her up and plopped her down in his ranch, moving with certainty while she dozed. Using his dimples when she faltered, Lucas had made her lose control of her life. She wanted it back and she wanted Lucas in it. Because he was an old-fashioned guy, loaded with hang-ups about modern relationships, she would have to marry him to soothe his inhibitions.

No other man had ever affected her the way Lucas could, making her feel alive and passionate, riding on the cusp of happiness so close she could taste its sweetness. While she sensed his fear of their relationship, she couldn't allow his shyness to crush the future she wanted.... When it came to Lucas, she was a very greedy woman.

Smoothing her stomach, Chastity smiled slightly. She'd love the fantasy to be true, to carry Lucas's child tucked within her.

The cold air hit her bare legs as Chastity slipped into the soft flannel robe and tied the sash with a jerk. She had been pushed enough. Lucas's worn moccasins looked warm and comfortable and she slid into them, padding across to open the door.

The three tall Walkingtons pivoted to her, their expressions tight with a temper she suspected was a family trait. "Okay, I'm awake now," she said warningly, meeting Lucas's scowl. "I'm not falling asleep at the drop of a hat anymore. I am fully, truly awake and I really don't like confrontations."

With a small degree of pride she acknowledged that she'd managed to keep her temper and voice controlled. "Hustling poor, sleepy Chastity into Oklahoma is kaput. My wedding day is next Saturday, Lucas. If you don't stop antagonizing these girls, you can forget playing the groom," she said, fighting the tug of warmth in her lower stomach as Lucas's dark gaze slowly prowled up her bare legs where the robe had separated.

She inhaled, drew herself up to every centimeter of her five-foot-six frame. She had once extracted Hope from a love-stricken, beefy wrestler using the same menacing technique. "Summer . . . Raven . . . if your father insists on marrying me—a sacrifice he seems honor-bound to make—then *I* insist that you act as bridesmaids at a church wedding. I've always said, if you're going to do something, do it right."

"It's Tuesday morning," he stated flatly. "It's four days until Saturday."

"I said I'm awake. You're not calling my tune on some royal male whim. That's four days of the couch for you," she returned hotly. Lucas had pushed enough; now it was her turn to set terms. A thrill raced through her—Lucas didn't want to be apart from her.

He was hers, and she was his, but there were rules. "I'm no longer so tired, Lucas. I believe that any decisions concerning our lives should be made jointly now. Isn't that right?" she challenged.

Raven giggled and hugged her father, who stared at Chastity blankly. "Dad, you should see your face," Raven chirped happily before Lucas stalked out the door and slammed it behind him.

Chastity smiled tightly, surprised at the simmering temper within her. Then she tightened the huge robe, shuffled the comfortable moccasins to the table and picked up a slice of toast. The girls stared as she nibbled on a corner and shot a dark look at the closed door. "That man," she muttered, "can be difficult."

"Yes," the girls echoed at once.

Chastity held up a firm finger. "But. He can be sweet."

"Uh-huh. Sure." The twins' tones lacked sincerity.

"Last night was the first time we've heard him laugh for years," Raven muttered.

Jerking the robe sash tighter, Chastity luxuriated in regaining her control. She nibbled on the toast and regretted the loss of poor, quiet, amendable Chastity. Lucas would roll over her like a bulldozer—she debated the term, "roll over her" and blushed. Lucas dismissed conventional romance with a sweep of his Stetson.

She wanted the whole enchilada with Lucas. She would drag love and romance out of him while he worked on old-fashioned obligation.

She wanted Lucas Walkington from his battered cowboy hat to his dusty boots.

Then she smiled the perfect smile, controlling both corners of her mouth to lift them equally.

"We'll work on your father's laughter. Tonight we'll work on the wedding, after your homework is done. Please tell your father on your way to school that he is to reserve the church for Saturday afternoon at one o'clock. I'm sure there is a white country church around here and that's where I want the wedding. I'm wearing white. A friend gave me her gown and veil and I'm wearing it.''

Chastity breathed deeply, power surging through her. Maybe it was the clean air in outer, greater Oklahoma. Or maybe it was Lucas Walkington, waiting to be challenged. She doubted that many women had challenged Lucas. He was in for one memorable experience. If he thought he could withhold romance and love from *her* marriage, he was off base. If she was pregnant, she wanted her baby to be in a real family embroidered with love. Chastity dusted crumbs from her hands and lifted her head. Lucas needed taming and she, Chastity Beauchamp, had found the challenge of her lifetime. ''I've always wanted a Saturday afternoon, one o'clock wedding. If the church isn't free this Saturday, then we'll wait for an opening. Your father is used to having his way. If I stay—if I marry him—things will have to change.''

''Go, Honey!'' the twins cheered.

Six

Lucas watched Chastity walk slowly toward the ancient oak tree that had marked Walkington land since his great-great-grandparents had settled on it.

Wearing loose cotton slacks and a city maxi-style coat, she looked tiny against the vast rolling prairie that baked in the summer and froze in the winter. The wind pushed at her, making her lean slightly against it while Wayne yipped and played at her side. Amid the dead stalks, new spring grass began to show, the March air heavy with the scent of the land just turned by his tractor plow and waiting to be seeded.

His cattle spread across a knoll, watching Chastity move toward that single huge oak reigning like a monarch over the land. Lucas ran his hand across Duke's muzzle as the horse whinnied, his nostrils catching the woman's scent.

Squinting against the early afternoon sun, Lucas stood trapped in the magic of inevitable time and his deep emotions. *He wanted her like that, walking straight and proud across the land of his birth, the land he hoped to leave his children.*

This morning she'd startled him, those green eyes hot with anger, challenging him on the spot.

Lucas patted the horse's muscled neck with his glove, pleased with Chastity's temper flash. With narrowed eyes, he traced her walk to a knoll, where she stood in the sunlight amid the sun and the wind as though she already belonged to the land... to him. He liked discovering that grit beneath the soft, loving ways. Liked that she wasn't afraid to put him in his place. Whatever he wanted from a woman it was the truth.

Alesha had walked to that same knoll, making her choice to leave him and take the girls to her parents'.

Three years of driving to Tulsa, spending two hours each weekend with his growing daughters, had stretched Lucas and his beat-up farm pickup to the limit. He'd lost four calves and three cows because of fatigue or because he wasn't there for them.

The twins were three when Alesha had called suddenly, asking him to take custody. She wanted a new life with a man who didn't want children. "The twins are just like you, Lucas. There's no possible way they can ever be civilized. I can't afford to throw my life away after them when they're never going to be anything but Walkington tomboys," she'd yelled. "I don't know why I ever spoiled my body bearing them...."

Lucas's jaw ached and he forced his teeth apart. His heart had been racing with the memory and the fear that Chastity would react as Alesha had years ago.

"Let's go see just where I stand with the lady now, boy," he murmured, tugging his hat down against the wind.

She stood against the old tree, surveying the miles of prairie, broken only by electric poles and dirt roads. The wind colored her cheeks, tugging strands of her hair free from the braid and curling them around the rough bark. She held a dried stalk of milkweed pods in her hand, her eyes almost closed.

In profile her jaw promised strength, her lips the softness of a woman, the gentle sweep of lashes the innocence of the child-woman he'd taken. "Hello, city woman," Lucas said softly as she watched his approach from those mysterious, half-closed eyes.

She smiled, enchanting him with the lift of those sweet lips at one corner. "Hello, cowboy."

Lucas shared the tree with her and wished she shared his life. "So you'll marry me Saturday. The church is free."

Her head turned slightly against the bark, eyes marking each feature of his face as though she were tucking it inside her forever. "Don't press your luck. I'm not happy with you now."

Gathering the coat closer to her, Chastity stared at his Angus cattle. "A temporary marriage isn't for me."

"Temporary?" Lucas fought the terror sweeping through him. His hand wrapped around her wrist, her pulse beat steadily beneath his fingertips. Shrugging her shoulder with elegant meaning, Chastity closed her eyes. "Annulment, divorce, estrangement. I've never stepped out on a ledge before, Lucas, and I'm frightened."

Twisting a wisp of silky hair around his dark finger, Lucas leaned closer. "You think I'm not?" he asked huskily, sensing that this moment would determine if she stayed with him.

When she lifted her head, her eyes were clear and green, filled with his reflection. "Lucas, people don't get married because of a fantasy weekend. They don't change the course of their lives on a whim, and they don't get married without love."

Pain shot through Lucas like a cold iron. His tense muscles ached. "I married once for love. It's a cow pile in the back lot."

"But you want a marriage?" she asked disbelievingly.

This time Lucas stared at his cattle. "I'm not a man who jumps around. I won't put my boots under any other woman's bed while I'm married to you."

"It isn't enough. There's tenderness and a partnership involved." Chastity's tone had risen defensively. "You acted impulsively, Lucas. A sense of honor won't be love, and you'll feel cheated in the end. You'll look at me one day and wonder how you could have married me. Now is the time to change your mind—"

He looked at her sharply. "Are you saying you're hightailing it back home?"

Her eyebrows shot up with the challenge. "I'm saying that you'd better think before marrying me, Lucas."

"Are you saying no?" he pressed, his heart aching with heavy, pounding heartbeats.

Her head tilted, her eyes focusing slowly on his face. He recognized the slow blink as though she missed her glasses. "Are you?"

"It's right, buttercup. You're what I want," he said tightly.

"That's nice," she returned in the same tone. "You're what I want."

"It will work," Lucas said finally, slowly, thinking how green her eyes were, how warm her lips were beneath his. *God, it had to work, but he couldn't give her love. Love for a woman wasn't in him. Alesha had taken his love and buried it in a nightmare.*

He leaned down, nuzzled the wind and sunlight tangled in her hair and prayed for the moment to last. "It's hard out here," he whispered as the wind tossed a curl against his cheek and it caught in the stubble he'd been too angry to shave. "Hard on women."

The Chicago pawnshop ring in his pocket was a good introduction to his finances. Thin, gold and hocked by someone needing cash, it bent Lucas's pride. He pictured placing a tiny diamond on his wife's slender fingers and the hurt went deeper. "What do you think about the place?" he asked, expecting a list of what she needed.

The small house and looming, ancient barn were surrounded by barbed-wire fences and electric poles zigzagging off into the horizon. Battered by time, the old windmill clattered away in the wind, a monument to his lost dreams.

Scanning the small frame house with a large back porch and larger front porch, Chastity's mouth eased into a tender, one-sided smile. "It's beautiful and warm. Like a jewel on a green ocean. Oh, Lucas, the air smells so clean." He liked that, sharing the timeless tree and the sun with her, her voice husky with sleep. Unable to resist, he turned her cheek with a finger and bent his head for a light kiss that lingered.

Her lips followed the gentle pursuit of his until Lucas asked, "Still mad at me?"

"You..." She searched for the word, her eyes half-closed and her breath washing sweetly across his lips.

He kissed her again. "Stir you up?"

The half smile returned and Lucas kissed its warmth. "Are you sorry?"

She leaned against him slightly, raising her face for his kisses like a kitten snuggling to a petting hand. "None of this makes sense, Lucas. There is no need for you to marry me. Nor to feel any obligation. I'm perfectly capable of handling my life, my way. I have no idea why I permitted you to take over.... Everything is happening too fast."

He chuckled at that and her lashes fluttered. "What?"

"Some things aren't happening enough," he teased as a fragrant curl slid across his lips.

"Lucas," she whispered in that sad way that made him ache everywhere. "Haven't you realized that I'm nothing like Honey?"

"Nope."

The sea-green eyes darkened and she breathed lightly. "You take my breath away."

"I'd like to. The girls are at school," he offered, testing his luck and sliding his hands beneath the heavy coat. Beneath it, she was round and soft, her waist an indentation that just fit his hands before they smoothed the flaring curve of her hips. He caressed her ribs, running his thumbs along the outer curve of her breast.

"Lucas, you are impossible," she whispered, desire flushing her cheeks.

"Hungry is the word, buttercup," he corrected, nibbling on her bottom lip with his teeth. His hand slid under her sweater and upward, caressing her breast. "It's cold out here," he murmured, thinking of the warmth of her body waiting for him.

He'd been cold for years, he realized suddenly as the sun tangled in her hair, the wind whipping it gently. He'd acted instinctively, grasping the woman who warmed him, who made him feel like a man.

Then she was curling against him, lifting her arms to lock behind his head. "Poor baby," she teased, the half smile dying as his aroused body locked with hers. Lucas cupped her hips, raising her to him hard. Heat shot between them, and Chastity's eyes widened in surprise. "My," she whispered.

He grinned when she shot a shy glance downward. "My goodness," she whispered, looking up at him.

A red-tailed hawk squealed overhead and a rabbit scampered into the brush. Wayne barked at sparrows and pranced about with a stick in his mouth. Rummaged by the wind, a dead leaf on the oak sifted down to settle at their feet.

Pushing his luck, Lucas slipped his hand to unhook her bra. Her breasts were soft, filling his hand with gentle weight as a blush began in her throat and worked up to her cheeks, flushed by the cold wind. "You're changing, buttercup. Ripening—"

"Goodness, Lucas, you make me feel like a tomato or a melon." Chastity buried her warm face against his throat and held his arms. "This is all so fast. My head is spinning."

Then he was kissing her, taking what he wanted, and her arms were locked around him, keeping the cold wind away. "I need you," he said roughly, meaning it. Then deeper, rougher, "You're mine."

Fear raced around him as Chastity raised her eyes slowly and they filled with his reflection. Lucas's stomach hurt, his heart pounding.

Then Chastity's soft mouth began to curl, that gentle mysterious smile snared him in a soft web, easing the terror. "Don't worry, babe," Chastity whispered, licking the dimple groove beside his mouth. "I'll take care of you."

Four days later in outer, greater Oklahoma in a small town named Chip for buffalo chip, Chastity spoke her wedding vows to a man she'd barely seen for days. Beside her Lucas wore his Western-cut, blue-gray church suit, and a grim expression.

Throughout the day and the country-style reception, he'd snapped at Summer and Raven, who were spending the weekend with a girlfriend. He barely noticed Chastity's gown, a soft white cotton with lace and long sleeves. When he jammed the thin gold band on her finger, his bitter expression had frightened her.

By eight o'clock that night, Chastity fought the simmering anger that had been brewing since he'd dropped her off in front of the house with a grim "Git."

"Git," Chastity muttered as she waited for her groom to complete the chores and stalk his cute little rear end to her wedding bed. In the four days she'd been dozing and getting acquainted with the Walkington family, she'd found that Lucas deeply loved his daughters, but didn't know how to communicate with them. Crossing her arms over the black lace peignoir, Chastity tapped her foot.

She closed her lids and remembered his worn wallet, Lucas opening it to pay the minister for the church, then turning to give his daughters each a bill. Because money had never mattered to Chastity, she found her pride scratched. Lucas could have used her savings, if she had them. She'd watched his mouth tighten and suddenly realized that the Walkington's trip to Chicago for her and the rented Suburban had cost money he could ill afford.

"Git," she repeated, jerking a cold-cut dinner from the refrigerator and plopping a bottle of red wine on the table. She sloshed the wine into a glass and glared at the lights in the barn as she sipped it. Husbands didn't keep to themselves. She would not have a husband who blew hot and cold in their relationship. He might be Mr. Lord of the Plains to his daughters, but he was just so much good-looking sweetcakes to her—he was a babe and he'd better not forget it. Babes had responsibilities to the women they chose to gift with their babe-ness. Like cuddling and—

At her feet, Wayne tilted his white curly head and whined sympathetically.

Striving to push down her rising anger, Chastity glanced around the Walkington home. Lucas's home was cozy, beautiful in its practical mix-and-match furniture. Her plants swallowed a corner by a window and her framed family pictures rested on a buffet that had crossed the plains in a covered wagon. A rocker that had belonged to Lucas's great-grandmother waited in the shadows to rock sleepy babies. She ran her finger around the Old Coot's picture lovingly. "You would have loved Oklahoma, Old Coot. It would be a real challenge. Lucas certainly is."

Sensible area rugs covered a gleaming hardwood floor; the big family kitchen with a washroom and pantry slid into a spacious living room. The gas cookstove and refrigerator were ancient, but a new washer-and-dryer set dominated the washroom. Surprised when she first learned that dishwashers weren't a standard household appliance, Chastity discovered that people in Oklahoma dried dishes on a rack-thing. Sometimes they dried clothing on lines strung from poles in the ground.

She sloshed wine into her empty glass and studied the clothes neatly arranged on hangers by the washer. Last night the washer and dryer had run past midnight, and she noted the basket of towels waiting to be folded. In the days prior to their wedding. Lucas had not made one move toward her, other than those dark blue eyes making promises that no righteous man could keep—she desperately wanted that wild, heated freedom of Lucas's lovemaking and it was her night to howl, darn it.

She rephrased that mentally, remembering the small, hungry noises she'd discovered she'd been making that night at Casa Bianca. The proper term was swooning noises. Maybe she had purred later.

Chastity plopped her glass on the table, jerked her maxi-coat from the hook in the pantry, grabbed a beer from the refrigerator and braced herself against the wind on the way to the barn.

He'd hustled her out of Chicago against her better judgment. If he changed his mind about trapping a plain woman in lieu of a goddess, he would have to tell her outright.

Lucas watched with interest as she fought the wind and the huge board door, finally opening it and squeezing through the narrow passage. "You could have used the door," he drawled, looking up from polishing his leather saddle.

"Door?" Chastity found it immediately and whirled to him, her anger raging. "I see no reason to dillydally, Lucas Walkington. 'Git' isn't a word that a groom uses to his bride on *their wedding night*." She tossed the beer to him and adjusted the maxi-coat around her with dignity, then plopped on a square hay-thing. A horse whinnied in the looming darkness of the barn and she jumped, frightened at the noise.

Lucas sipped the beer and leaned against the rail, which supported his saddle. "What's up? You look like you're in a tizzy."

"Tizzy?" The casual remark caused Chastity to narrow her eyes at him. "You've been hiding out for days, Lucas. Avoiding me. That romantic kiss at the wedding may have fooled the others, but it didn't me. You've changed your mind and should be man enough to admit it. You've found yourself in a mess with a woman that doesn't suit you and are taking your punishment like a man." She jerked her thumb to her chest. "*I* don't want to be that punishment. That cross to bear...that albatross around your neck, the old lady—"

His eyes slid from her face to the part in the coat, then down the long length of her legs. She inhaled sharply, fighting her temper and the rising need to— "Typically a groom is interested in his bride on their wedding night, Lucas," she reminded him stiffly, looking at him from his arrogant black hair to the tip of his polished, dress boots.

She pushed back a bobbing curl that detracted from her forceful impact. His light blue shirt was open low and a bit of pink confetti nestled in the crisp hair covering his chest. Chastity closed her eyes against the hot wave of desire taking her breath. "Being dropped like a stinky sock doesn't do much for a girl's ego on her wedding night," she said, her words dropping off into the barn's spacious gloom.

"Uh-huh. I said you'd have to ask. What are you wearing under that thing?" he asked, placing his beer aside to walk toward her. Lucas stood over her, forcing her to look up. The stark light of the single bulb swaying overhead hit his grim expression, changing his face into sharp planes and dark shadows. A tense muscle moved on his upper cheek, running down into the dark shadows of his evening beard. "Marriage can be hell," he stated in a cold tone that cut Chastity's heart, as though speaking his thoughts out loud. "I promised myself I'd never step in that cow pile again. There wasn't much left of me after the last time. That ring you're wearing is pure pawnshop."

Uncertain of his mood, Chastity watched his face harden, his hand reaching out to wrap in her curls. "All this is natural, isn't it?'' he questioned in the same musing tone. "You've got a few cosmetics in the bathroom. *All* of you is natural, isn't it?''

"Oh, Lucas," she whispered, her throat tightening with emotion. "I'm not a bit like Honey. I'm just practical, plain old me. Except my hair was layered and lightened for the show and now it won't stay in my braids. It's a curse. I think annulment might be in order if you've changed your mind, and I think you should.''

His hands wrapped in the coat's lapels, drawing her to her feet. "You keep reminding me that you're not Honey. Why did you come out here?''

"Out here in Oklahoma, or out here in the barn?''

The warm fingertip prowling her hot cheek slid to her earlobe and tugged. "The barn. I didn't give you much rope to do anything but come to the ranch with me.''

"I made that decision myself, thank you," she returned loftily. There was danger dancing in his blue eyes, challenging her. Chastity's body ached, his heat and scents driving into her. Then she caught the amusement flickering beneath his lashes and it set her off. The muscles in her cheek locked with anger. "I came to thank you for the nice time today, Lucas. I loved meeting the people of Chip. That's why.''

"Uh-huh. I don't buy that.''

Chastity stood, too filled with anger to care about the consequences. He wanted the truth slapped across his hidden dimples, did he?

She jerked open the maxi-coat, dropped it to the hay and pushed Lucas's chest hard with her open hands. "You jerk. I came because I wanted you. Because wedding nights are supposed to be romantic, simmering with romance. But oh, no. I spent a full hour in the bathroom, waiting for my impatient groom to tap on the door. But oh, no, not this groom—'' With that she poked his chest. "But now I've changed my mind," she stated airily, reaching to replace the coat. "It's your loss," she managed with as much dignity as a woman who has offered herself and met rejection.

The tiny straps supporting the black gown snapped easily beneath Lucas's hands and it slipped, pooling at her feet. Grabbing the transparent negligee closer, Chastity scowled at Lucas. "Babe, that wasn't nice."

Her hopes for the evening soared higher. Tearing her clothing off was just the right cure to her unstable, wild emotions. She needed to know that he wanted her as desperately as she wanted him.

"I love it when you get tough, buttercup," he drawled, running a finger around the dark tip of her breast and watching with interest as it peaked. He bent to kiss it through the sheer material without laying a hand on her. While Chastity dealt with the melting hunger skimming down her body and circling in her lower stomach, he grinned wickedly and the dimples appeared.

She pushed at his chest again, wanting to physically... physically do something. To show him she wasn't a simpering woman of yesteryear, Chastity took his lapels in both hands and jerked his shirt apart. Buttons flew into the barn dust, clinking and rolling and setting her temper aflame. She hadn't ever really exposed the world to the temper she controlled, but Lucas Walkington—her alleged groom—was testing her to the limits. "This is my wedding night, sweetcakes, and I want the whole enchilada."

Deep inside her, sweet little shy Chastity Beauchamp, shivered in confusion. Reaching out and taking wasn't in her gentle nature.

Chastity Walkington decided that lust was a good place to start. Wrangling Lucas into committing his heart was a serious matter and she intended to turn on the heat.

She thought of the heat she'd experienced twice and started to sizzle.

"My, my," he drawled, flicking a glance down at her nails, which had been gently clawing his chest. That hungry, dark blue stare at her body stroked Chastity's ego like a match to tinder. Throwing away caution, Chastity allowed the negligee to slide to the floor, leaving her standing pale and nude beneath the stark lighting.

Lucas's gaze slid down her curves slowly, intently.

"This barn isn't heated, is it?" she asked uneasily. No man had taken her apart inch by inch, making her feel soft, feminine and desirable as a beautiful woman. Now Lucas inspected every trembling inch with deep interest.

"You're not lean," he said quietly, inspecting her breasts, which had started to ache for the warmth of his mouth. He traced her stomach, and Chastity fought her blush as he stared intently at the shadows above her inner thighs.

To her distress, the soft flesh quivered.

"No. I've never thought diets were sensible," she said tightly, intensely aware that she stood unclothed, bared to his scrutiny, while he remained fully dressed.

She wanted him stripped and in bed. Chastity glanced around the shadowy barn.

"Bed isn't the only place I'll want to make love, buttercup," Lucas drawled as though he followed her thoughts. He watched her expressions, then reached to tug the light bulb's string and the barn went dark.

Maybe the pickup truck's bed? she offered silently, desperately wanting his heat, wanting that exquisite joining of his body with hers. *Or the pickup's long front seat?* Good Lord, where did people in Oklahoma make love?

When he chuckled, toying with a curl swirled around his fingers, Chastity glared up at him. "You're enjoying this, babe."

"You got that right, buttercup. Your expressions tell me just what you're thinking. It's pretty complimentary to have a lady come calling—"

"Hush," Chastity ordered sharply. "And lay down on those square hay-things—"

"Bales—bales of hay," Lucas said when he stopped grinning that devastating, all-cocky, arrogant, desirable male grin.

"Whatever. Git. Just do it." Good Lord, if she didn't have him near her, holding her, wrapped around her soon, she would burst.... "You are a difficult man, Lucas Walkington," she said, her words sliding off into the howl of the night wind as he began undressing.

Placing his shirt carefully beside her coat on the hay bales, Lucas reached into the back of the pickup and shook out a blanket. "Make-do," he explained simply, covering the bales.

"Lay down, sweetcakes," she ordered tightly, needing him desperately. Clearly her body wouldn't allow her to be the blushing, reluctant partner. Lucas seemed to enjoy her ploy and, encouraged, Chastity pushed him slightly.

His broad back tensed, the muscles rippling. Straightening, Lucas unfastened his belt and slacks and shucked his shorts in the process, presenting her with a wonderful view of broad shoulders and ridges and cute little dimples low on his spine. She touched a devastating little indentation experimentally and the sheer need to swathe his body with hers enveloped her. He stood tensed as she swept her palm over the ridges and planes of his shoulder, skimming the muscles of his upper arms. Her tiny, awed gasp and the sound of her heavy heartbeat filled the airy barn.

"You're the boss," Lucas said in a low, husky, uneven tone. "What now?"

"Lay down—no...." Chastity wrapped her arms around him, and pressed her body to his back. It was warm and deliciously hard. Then, without mooring, her palms slipped a little on his flat stomach and she jerked her hands back, flushing as she realized there was an anchor of sorts available. "Ohh!"

Lucas moved forward suddenly, unbalancing her and turning to catch her as she sprawled over him on the bales. He locked her to him with one arm, cupping her bottom with his hand, while his other hand prowled her curves. Taking his time, Lucas lifted her breast to his mouth, licked the area around the center and whispered against her skin, "I'm here. Now what are you going to do with me?"

Fighting to think, to stop the coils of desire centering low in her stomach, she clung to his shoulders with all her strength.

"This?" he asked, lifting his hips slightly and easing into her. "Or this...." Then she was filled, heated, pulsing around him.

Moments later, she lay draped over Lucas's warm body, the coat covering her as he waited for her to recover. He chuckled in her ear. "That was some compliment."

She roused long enough to whisper against his dark warm throat. "What?"

"I turn you on, buttercup. You were already on the edge, waiting for me. A man likes to know he's attractive for his wife. What do we do now?" She sensed the humor, the deep hunger riding him, the tense muscles of his thighs lifting slightly to press deeper within her.

"Oh, Lucas, I don't know anything about this wife business. I don't know anything about raising a family, or your daughters, or—" His kiss stopped her.

"One thing at a time," he whispered in the dark, rolling gently over her. "Let's work on finishing the current project.... Tell me what you want next..."

Then he moved deeply within her and Chastity knew what she wanted.

Later Chastity was surprised to find that her babe knew how to walk and make love, too. The process was incredibly erotic. Lucas swathed her in her coat, ordered her to lock her legs around him and stood with her in his arms. At the barn door, she couldn't stop the quiet scream of pleasure.

He was naked and magnificent, his body damp and cold as he entered the night. She whimpered softly again when he opened the house door. Then Lucas placed her on the washer. Chastity looked at his stark features, at the slightly swollen curve of his bottom lip, and moved closer to him. She nestled her breasts against his hairy chest and luxuriated in the rough texture. "I can wait until we're in a bed," Lucas said tightly as she bent to lick his nipple, suckling it gently as he had her.

The challenge was too much. Chastity launched herself at him, determined to keep their beautiful joining through the night. "Don't leave me, babe," she whispered before tracing the whorls of his ear with the tip of her tongue.

"Oh, damn," he whispered hoarsely, gathering her closer and moving with her flow. Minutes or an eternity later, Lucas cuddled Chastity's warm, limp body with big, unsteady hands. "We just made love on the washer, buttercup." He sounded incredulous.

She nestled in his arms, biting his shoulder sleepily. She'd really gotten the hang of loving Lucas and though part of her wanted to play into eternity, part of her wanted to roll herself around him and sleep. "The dryer is close. You wouldn't have to carry me far...."

Lucas snorted at that. Chastity had the impression that she had bruised his dignity, his ability to control the moment. That sound reached into her ego and jerked it two stories high. "Let's eat," she whispered, suddenly filled with energy that had escaped her for over a month.

"Eat. I'm lucky to be breathing," Lucas stated in a dark, irritated growl and glared at the washer. "Git," he ordered Wayne, who was watching with interest. The dog sulked into Summer's room to hide.

Elated with her first success as Mrs. Walkington, Chastity patted his stubbly cheeks and kissed the lips that responded nicely to her nibbling prompts. "Sweetcakes, there are cold cuts on the table. I'll be right back."

He snared her wrist and stayed her for a moment, reluctant to let her go. Chastity loved the uncertain, primitive, incredulous, macho expressions shifting beneath his dark skin. She truly loved the wary look in his blue eyes; he seemed dazed by her attempts at passion. She hummed in the shower and got that little peremptory rap on the door that she had wanted earlier.

"Yes?" she asked innocently, studying the chafe marks Lucas's beard had made in the steamy mirror. "Who is it?" A snort of male disgust raised her hopes for a lovely evening. Lucas entered the small room when she opened the door, shot a wary glance at her and stepped into the shower.

Lucas Walkington, Oklahoma babe, was just the man she'd been waiting to try out all her life. That thought warmed her through their brief candlelight dinner. Wearing a pair of worn jeans, open at the waist, Lucas concentrated on his cold-cut sandwich. A deep flush of red ran up his tanned cheeks when he glanced at her breasts covered by another gown with tiny straps. Chastity slathered mustard on her sandwich while little pings of pleasure shot off inside her. No doubt Lucas was thinking of the straps he'd torn earlier. "I'm thirty-eight," he said suddenly, startling her. "A man takes pride in his control."

His eyes jerked down to her bosom and lingered in the deep crease covered by black lace and pink satin. "You are one well-developed woman. Hungry, too."

Chastity chewed on her sandwich and his comment. She decided it was a compliment and that he liked her curvaceous body. In a few words, he'd erased the lifelong doubt she'd had about her sensuality. She didn't feel pink-pastel sweet and blushing bride-like; she felt like a beautiful, redhot, desirable woman. The passion humming through her like electricity skimmed along her skin, and she wanted to toss Lucas's six-foot-three body on the floor and have her wicked way with him. Whatever happened between them later, she was having a wonderful, exhilarating wedding night to remember forever. She loved the stunned expression in his blue eyes as she stood and slipped the gown off, tossing it to a chair. Lucas stared at the tiny black-lace strip serving as briefs, then up at the hunger in her expression. "Lady, you are really asking for it," he warned as she slid onto his lap.

Closing her eyes, Chastity thought how she'd like to try with Lucas all the sensual how-to's she'd read about in contemporary magazines. Lucas sucked in his breath as her fingers wandered over him, testing the zipper— "Easy. That could be dangerous," he warned sharply when she tugged it experimentally.

She nestled on him, squirmed to get more comfortable on his hard body and grinned when his hand slid to cup her breasts. He trembled then, his fingers smoothing the lace covering her heat. "You're ready again, aren't you?" he asked in a startled tone, as though speaking his thoughts aloud.

"Just for you," she urged desperately. "Oh, Lucas, take me now."

They were on the couch suddenly, the springs creaking with their joined weight. Lucas's jeans opened magically while Chastity kissed him on the mouth—she loved the taste of Lucas on her tongue. Then she was settling down on his aroused length and in a quick jerk, Lucas tore away the lace separating them.

"I think we're going to have to work on our timing—like taking things nice and easy," he murmured as he scooped her up later. Chastity poured her well-sated body into his keeping and snuggled into his arms.

At the doorway to his bedroom, she threw out a hand and caught the doorframe, bracing a foot against it, stopping him. She asked the question that had tormented her for days. "Lucas, I have to know. Did you share that bed with your wife?"

"No." He eased her through the doorway and stood holding her, his body tense. "Bought it at an auction. The mattress and springs are new. Got them before coming to get you."

"Good enough." Chastity didn't want to know anything else. She just wanted to sleep, wrapped in Lucas's safe arms.

Something hard and warm shifted beneath Chastity, rousing her as the catcalls, car horns and pounding began. Lucas rumbled and growled, pushing his chest against her breasts. He snorted and lurched and reached out to hold her protectively against him. She turned her head slightly on the pillow to watch Lucas awake with a curse. He wiped his hand across his face, blinked several times and snatched the clock from the bedside table, holding it near his face. "Damn. I'm too old for a shivaree."

"Shivaree?" she asked, aware of the instant heat between them.

Lucas shot a hard look at her, eased from beneath her leg and tugged her arm gently from him. "Just a lot of sh— manure. People with nothing to do stand around and harass newlyweds—" He stopped, glanced down at her grin as though surprised.

"That's right, Lucas. You qualify as a newlywed."

"I'm a little past the prime picture," he shot back, then ran a possessive hand down her backside, cupping her bottom.

The hooting and banging grew louder, circling the house. Wayne barked and bounded up on the bed. He stood on Lucas's flat stomach, clearly defending his master. Car lights cut through the curtains. "Hey, Lucas! Whatcha doin'?" a man called out as the noise rose above the howling wind. "Come on out and say howdy," another man yelled.

"Hey, Lucas, remember the time you shivareed me and my Betsy? Your turn now."

A woman's voice slid through the night. "Git on out here, Lucas Walkington. We've got the wheelbarrow ready...."

Lucas continued a steady stream of curses, standing up and jerking a clean pair of jeans from the closet. He paused, ran his hands over Chastity's clothing next to his and shook his head as if dazed.

"Hey, Lucas! You left the barn door open. Guess what I found inside," a younger man yelled.

"That would be James Lexington—"

"Daddy? We're waiting." Summer's voice swept into the room. "Time to push the wheelbarrow."

Lucas shook his head. "That girl is going to get her backside paddled—"

"Lucas, my old bones can't stand this night wind much longer. Get yourself out here now," an older woman demanded.

"Hattie McCord. Tough as old leather," Lucas muttered. He glanced at Chastity, who had snuggled down to watch his warring emotions. "Get up. They won't leave us alone until we pay our dues."

"I'm too comfortable. You go." She grinned, snuggled down deeper in the quilt and sniffed the pleasant scent of his body on the bedding. "I'm tired."

His grin was slow, disarming and deep with dimples. Scooping her from the bed, Lucas tossed her lightly in his arms and said, "Are you getting dressed or do you want the whole countryside to see you in the raw?"

"You wouldn't." Chastity's smile died as he began to walk toward the living room. She caught the doorframe a second time that night. "Stop. What do I wear?"

He lowered her to her feet and patted her backside. "Anything, a pair of jeans. Get a move on. I want some sleep tonight."

"I don't have jeans. What about cotton slacks and a sweater? Or maybe a matching blouse and skirt? Or . . . "

"This isn't a fashion show, Mrs. Walkington. It's a damned circus," Lucas snapped impatiently. Then Chastity caught the dark hunger in his eyes before he shielded it.

Skimming down his body, she noted the heavy arousal thrusting at his worn jeans. Because he was in a snit, impatient and arrogant, Chastity wriggled slowly into cotton slacks and a sweater. Lucas needed tempering and when she looked over her shoulder at him, his face was dark with desire.

He might hide his love away, protect it ferverently, but he desired her and for now it was enough.

Minutes later, the wind swirled Chastity's hair around her as Lucas tucked her close to his side. Wayne bounced from friend to friend, holding court happily. Spotlights pinned them, cowbells rang, and wooden spoons banged on pots. "To the barn and back," the crowd ordered in a chant.

He squinted against glaring headlights. "Hey. I'm an old man. I've got two of the orneriest daughters this side of Tulsa. Save this stuff for the kids—"

A man's barroom voice cut through the wind. "Are you saving it?"

"Hell, he had to go across three states to get him a woman. He's scared all the rest off. He's been saving it for years," Hattie McCord taunted.

"Maybe I'm not anymore," Lucas returned smugly and Chastity hoped the wind would account for her hot flush. He bent to kiss her passionately, lifted her high in the air and swirled her around until she grasped at his bare shoulders. "We're having us a baby. No reason to go careful now."

"Oh dear, oh my," Chastity whispered between her well-kissed lips when the horns stopped and the crowd's eyes swung at her, pinpointing the area of her flat stomach beneath the coat.

Then Lucas laughed outright, the wind whipping at him, his face dark with a new beard.

The noise and the catcalls continued until Lucas placed her in a wheelbarrow and began pushing it toward the barn. Cattle lowed in the distance and a drop of rain touched Chastity's cheek as she held tightly to the bouncing old wheelbarrow. The crowd cheered loudly, confetti mixed with the light rain, and Chastity forced a wide smile.

Lucas had a few things to learn. Like waiting for a doctor's examination. Like asking her if she wanted the entire world to know she'd grabbed him in Casa Bianca.

Lucas ordered Summer to take Wayne, then pushed Chastity back to the house. He scooped her into his arms and ran into the bedroom, kicking the door shut.

Seven

———

Lucas's grin slowly died. Shimmering in volcanic fury, Chastity leaped to the bed, placed her hands on her hips and glared down at him. Her curls bobbed, glistening in the dim light as she stepped around the tumbled bedding. She pointed her finger at him. "You. You are the most infuriating man, Lucas Walkington."

Alarmed, Lucas snared her wrist only to be shaken loose. "Honey, be careful. You could hurt—"

"The baby, Lucas? The baby we don't know medically exists? The baby you just announced to the entire city of Chip?" she demanded in a soft explosion.

"Get down. You could hurt yourself," Lucas ordered tightly, but Chastity was past listening.

"Sweetcakes, don't you know that people actually converse, decide together about tossing personal information around Oklahoma?"

Unaccustomed to being dressed down, Lucas narrowed his eyes, staring the few inches up to her face. "I called it. I stand by it."

For a moment her eyes widened as she digested his statement. Then her chin jutted out and she snapped her fingers. "Huh. Just like that. You decided to inform everyone about something so...so personal. Don't you know that anybody with a brain can...?" She floundered a bit, slashing out her hands as a blush rose from her throat to her cheeks.

She kicked a pillow, looked at it, then bent to scoop it up and throw it at him. Lucas caught it and dropped it to the floor, uncertain about the illogical creature who had just thrown another pillow at his head. He dodged it, shot her a scowl that always calmed his daughters, and waited for the tempest to cool down. It didn't.

"I have to face everyone and they'll all be wondering. No, they'll *know* that I dragged you into bed right away. You just flopped it out in public. You just stood there and... Oh, this is really wonderful. Now everyone will know that you married me because you felt duty-bound—"

"Shot the honeymoon to hell, didn't it?" Lucas grated out.

She blinked, frowning. "What do you mean?"

He pushed his hands in his back pockets to keep them from trembling, fearing the worst. "I did something you don't like. Therefore, logically, it's the couch for me. Or a cold back." Chastity stared at him blankly, jammed her glasses on and leaned closer to see his face. "I don't know what you mean."

He smiled tightly with the fear racing inside him. Happiness wasn't meant to last a lifetime. "I've been through this routine before. Wife gets ticked and sex is out the door."

"Sex?" Chastity's voice was low, uneven and dangerous. The sea-green eyes shimmered with tears. "You think this is a matter of sex? Ohh!"

Then she was in front of him, thrusting her hands at his chest. "I want you to know that I have never...ever lost my temper. I've always used reason... You are impossible, Lucas Walkington." With that, Chastity reached up, grabbed his ears and tugged him down for a hard kiss. Her tongue pushed inside his mouth and she bit his lip before stepping away.

Lucas faced a trembling, angry woman who asked, "There. Does that feel like I'm ready to turn you away when you act like a...a yahoo?"

He tested his burning lip with his finger and tried to keep the foolish grin inside, warming away the fear.

"Sex!" she continued hotly, throwing out her hands. "Oh no, you couldn't say making love, or lovemaking. No, you said sex. Well, I've got news for you, Lucas. I like..." He noted with satisfaction that a rosy blush spread across her face.

He eased a clinging curl away from her cheek and she swatted his hand away. Taking a deep breath, Chastity said tightly, "You and I will talk—repeat—talk about personal things before we spread them from here to China. I've noticed serious gaps in our relationship. While I'm at it, since we're going to be a family, let's get some things straight."

Fascinated, Lucas watched while Chastity began to pace the length of the room, concentrating as she undressed, tossing her sweater at him as she passed. "This cow thing and horses. I want to understand farm life better, but if you keep sulking and hiding and working and staying away from me, I won't learn anything. Listen up, Lucas. I'm only going to let you keep pressure-lipped for so long—"

"That's 'tight-lipped,' honey," he corrected quietly from the shadows.

Chastity kicked off her shoes and glared at him, continuing as though she were Sherman marching through Georgia. "Then there's the matter of the girls."

She paused, unsnapped her cotton slacks, stepped out of them and tossed them to him. The soft quiver of flesh above her bra drew Lucas's attention. His jeans were suddenly uncomfortably tight as she continued. "We're getting to know each other and you're avoiding the inevitable. Those girls want to date and they will eventually. In the short time I've been in the Walkington family, I can see there is work to be done in your relationships. You're all so alike."

Chastity ignored his snort of disbelief. She unhooked her bra, slid free and flopped it over his shoulder. "The thing is, we've got a task cut out for us, and if there's one thing I'm good at, it's making lists. Well...there's that one other thing that I can do, but it's not important...a little gift I inherited from the Old Coot, but haven't really put to the test."

Lucas caught her discarded briefs, wrapping his hand in the warmth. "I've never been extremely passionate, or self serving. *Or violent.* But you set me off, Lucas Walkington," she muttered, glancing at him. "I never show temper and I'm always considerate of others almost to a fault. I wanted you and went after you. You were the first thing that I've ever wanted selfishly, without reservation. I liked— correct that—*like* how you make me feel...feminine and desirable. Oh..."

Chastity yawned, looked down at her socks and sat wearily on the bed. She yawned again, and murmured drowsily, "A garden. I want a real garden with big, fat juicy tomatoes and cucumbers, maybe snow peas and bok choy. Maybe kumquats or kiwis. Definitely mushrooms in that old root cellar."

Lucas swallowed the wad of emotion tightening his throat. He knelt slowly and began peeling off her socks, aware that she watched him drowsily. Her fingers combed through his hair soothingly, and with a sigh, she bent to kiss him. "My, I've never spoken like that to anyone. You're marvelous for inhibitions, Lucas. A real pressure valve. Thank you for listening, though I'm still rather angry about your announcement. I wanted a doctor's exam to back up the test—I feel glorious, Lucas." She was asleep before he lowered her head to the pillow.

Lying near Chastity, remaining still as her soft thigh crept between his and her arm began sliding across him, Lucas breathed shallowly. In moments, the soft fragrant curve of feminine body would begin inching over him.

His tears surprised him, warm on his lashes. Whatever, whoever Chastity was, she clearly wasn't tossing him out of her bed. Nor were her demands unreasonable.

He swallowed, shifting more comfortably as Chastity pushed her face into the hollow of his throat and shoulder. She nuzzled him and purred.

Not once in her tirade had the lady mentioned money, or rather, lack of. She wanted to learn about cows.

A soft curl caught on his beard, swirling its clean fragrance around him. Lazily caressing the sweep of his wife's back, Lucas fought the swell of emotion pressing against his chest.

Everything was just too damn good. It couldn't last.

He dozed, cuddling Chastity's soft body against him. Lucas awoke from his passion-filled dream to find himself already sheathed within her, her lips nibbling hungrily at his....

After his morning chores on Monday, Lucas packed Chastity into his pickup and drove fifteen miles to Chip. While Lucas pointed out various ranches, Chastity absorbed the tone of his voice, the deep pride and love ringing through it. Country music played from the radio, and somewhere in outer Oklahoma a boy advertised for his lost dog with brown spots and a mangled ear. Chastity sat close to Lucas, ignoring his grim expression and let Oklahoma seep into her bones. A vast state, filled with various Native American nations, it resembled Chicago's mixed nationalities.

The local supermarket was a combination gas station and feed store, since most residents purchased groceries forty miles away at a larger town. While Chastity hunted for broccoli, cauliflower, grapes and tofu, Lucas loaded grain sacks into the pickup. "What's wrong?" he asked, noting her few purchases as he took the basket from her.

"Lucas, they don't have pasta. Spaghetti and basic macaroni, but there's not a package of linguine anywhere. *Lucas, there's no fresh pasta. Not even tortellini. Where's the fresh-fish counter?"*

He tossed a package of spaghetti into the basket, his expression wary and grim. "This is meat-and-potato country, city girl. Most folks do their heavy shopping in Muggins. Beef and pork are in the freezer on our back porch. Fish are out in the lake waiting for a hook."

"A hook?" she screamed softly as Nellie Blackfeather grinned nearby. "They don't net them?"

Lucas shot a dark stare at Zeke Farris, who was snickering by the vegetable oil. "You want that garden? The onion sets and planting potatoes are over there. Get whatever seed you want. There's not much free water in the summer, so keep that in mind." He wandered off, pushing a dinky grocery cart with one bad wheel.

Chastity scooped onion sets to her heart's delight, then moved down the rows of bulk seed, filling tiny brown sacks with spinach, beans, lettuce and cucumber seed. A young pregnant woman with one child on her hip and holding a toddler's hand suggested that Chastity wait to purchase the cabbage and tomato plants that would arrive soon. "You're Lucas Walkington's new wife, aren't you?" she asked, kissing the ten-month-old baby straddling her hip, and tugging the toddler away from the bin of potatoes. She smiled shyly, her Native American features timeless and beautiful. "I'm Melody Bearclaw."

"Hi, Melody. Yes, I'm Lucas's wife." Little pings started shooting off in Chastity's stomach when she looked at the girl's rounded stomach. Then she knew—this baby may have startled them, but the next Walkington child wouldn't. She wanted children with Lucas—black hair, blue eyes, with streaks of pride running deep.

Meanwhile, he had lessons to learn.

She found Lucas instantly, standing a head above the aisle display and studying fabric softener. He tipped his hat back with his thumb, his black brows meeting as he concentrated.

"You've got your work cut out for you," Melody whispered with a grin. "He's been dodging women for years. Except for the things he attends with the twins, he'd hole up on that spread forever. No one could believe he entered that Lonesome Cowboy contest, or that he went to Chicago. I'm so happy for you. Lucas must have known what he wanted right away, with the baby coming so soon."

Chastity smiled warmly, meeting Lucas's sky blue eyes across the aisle. She wanted to pelt him with the onion sets and drag him behind the sacks of cow feed and lecture him on starting gossip. "We're not exactly certain about the baby."

Melody's grin widened. "If Lucas snatched you that quickly, he knew a good thing when he saw it. It's all so romantic. He's so proud of you. Goodness, I didn't think Lucas Walkington would ever marry. He's been like a wily old wolf for years. I heard the Walkington twins took away the ladder from the hayloft and stranded him until he agreed to listen to their idea about the Lonesome Cowboy contest." Lucas's expression shifted into arrogance as he smiled quickly, flashing his dimples.

Chastity returned the smile with a challenge. A dimple display over fabric softeners did not wash away his premature announcement. "Drop over for coffee, Melody. I'd love to learn more about Lucas."

The girl erupted in giggles. "I've never seen him smile, or look that innocent. . . . He's such a babe."

"A regular sweetcake," Chastity added darkly and plopped her basket on the counter. The owner and clerk, John Blue Sky, shot an appraising glance at her stomach.

The cart with the rattling wheel banged into the counter and Lucas glared at the change John had counted into her hand. "After this, John, if my wife wants anything, add it to my bill."

Scratched by Melody's reminder of Lucas's bold announcement at their shivaree, Chastity reached down to pinch his hard bottom. He jerked away, scowling. "I'm not without funds, Lucas dear." While Lucas's blue eyes promised revenge, John laughed. "Looks like you got a whole houseful of women now. Forgot something, didn't you, Lucas?"

"Yes, his coupons," Chastity said firmly. "Lucas, where are the coupons?"

He snorted and met John's amused eyes over her head. "He means something else."

Cursing softly, Lucas stalked down the aisle containing over-the-counter medications and returned with packages of feminine supplies. He jerked out a few bills and tossed them to the counter, slapped the worn wallet shut and jammed it into his back pocket. His grim determination not to show embarrassment caused Chastity to giggle and temporarily forgive his abrupt behavior at the store as they walked to the pickup. She scooted next to him, edged beneath his arm and grinned. "You're cute, Lucas Walkington. I bet you can't drive this pickup and kiss me, too."

He lifted a speculative eyebrow. "You keep it up, Miss Sass, and we'll likely to end—" He sucked in his breath as she snuggled close to him and caressed his thigh. . . .

Raising himself off her later, Lucas looked stunned. He peered out the steamy pickup windshield and swore. "We're parked behind Fanny Simmon's barn like a couple of over-heated kids."

The day was wonderful, brimming with sunshine and discoveries as Lucas wheeled the tractor into the yard and turned over the old family garden that hadn't been used for years. Chastity slipped off her shoes as she had been aching to do and experimented with the damp spring earth. It was soft and unbelievable. She wiggled her toes and sighed, smiling up at Lucas, who had been watching her. "I've never put my feet on real dirt," she explained shyly.

Chicago did have dirt, but not the freshly tilled, waiting-to-be-nourished soil. Lucas watched her, his eyes shadowed by the brim of his hat. For a moment, their eyes locked, tenderness flowing between them. The tangible emotion swirled around in the clean sunshine, warming her. "Barefoot and pregnant," Lucas said quietly. "You are a sight, Chicago lady."

She wanted to hold him, to wrap her arms around him and soothe away the pain that always seemed near him. Whatever his scars were, they ran deep. Another woman had shared him, wounded him and taken the love Chastity wanted desperately.

She eased her toes into the cool soft soil. Then something wiggled beneath Chastity's sole and she screamed. Lucas laughed outright when Chastity spotted another earthworm in the freshly turned earth. "Night crawlers," he explained, fascinated as she picked a cautious path to him.

"Snakes. Baby snakes, Lucas." With that she leapt for him as though he were a safe tree in a swamp filled with alligators. Lucas's laughter didn't stop until he lowered her to the ground.

"Those snakes are fishing worms. There's crappie and bluegill down at the lake." Then his lips tightened, his gaze lifted to the swelling horizon. "On the old place."

She sensed pain, running deep, swirling around him with memories, and waited for him to explain. Lucas looked down at her, the lines deepening in the shadows beneath his hat. "We're short of water here. Keep the garden small. The stock takes every drop in the summer. I'm helping Seth Jones lay fence until nightfall. The girls will be back after school. Better rest."

Then he shrugged and walked toward the barn, locking her away from him. Chastity stared at the closed door and knew that though Lucas shared his body with her, he wasn't sharing anything else. "Lucas Walkington, you are packing around a big bundle of pain by your little old lonesome."

That night Chastity turned her backside to the bedroom mirror and studied the tight-fitting Western jeans. A bridal present from Summer and Raven, they were perfect. They were worth every squirm, lying flat on the bed to squeeze into them. The girls explained how it was important to start Western jeans tight so that they wouldn't sag after wear.

Working as a team in the kitchen, Lucas and the girls had shooed her away. Chastity drew her hair up into a ponytail. She fastened it with a rubber band, then thrust combs into the sides to keep her hair from curling. The jeans protested tightly as she tied her joggers and stepped into the living room.

"You look great," Raven exclaimed, running to Chastity and turning her around. "Doesn't she, Daddy?"

Lucas straightened to his full height, his eyes flicking over her. "Whose damn idea was that?"

Wayne whined once, quietly, then slid off to his cushion near the couch.

"Stop cursing, Lucas," Chastity ordered softly as both girls turned toward him, their eyes filled with tears. If he wanted to point out her plainness to her, he could have chosen another time. "I'm probably not built right, anyway. Jeans look best on the leggy, lean type."

"You're built just fine. That's the problem," Lucas stated stiffly, placing a huge beef roast on the table. The meat had been simmering in a slow cooker all day and Chastity swallowed, suddenly aware that hunk of cooked, red meat was dinner. She closed her eyes and tried not to think of Rosebud's beautiful big brown eyes and long lashes.

"Daddy is old-fashioned, Chastity," Raven said in a bitter tone. "He won't let us date until our senior year in high school. That's only five months away, and Mel Jones wants to take me out now."

"Mel Jones." Lucas snapped the words between his teeth. "He wants to take you out drag racing on Melody Flats."

Raven lifted her chin. "To a movie, Dad. In Muggins."

"No."

Summer shot a dark look at Chastity. "All Daddy thinks about is money, grades and college. We want to be like everyone else. Just because he had to sell off part of the farm to keep this and couldn't go to college doesn't mean we have to live like prisoners. We're the only kids in school who still have to be home early after a game."

"'Prisoners.'" Lucas's snort indicated he wasn't investing time in the matter. Clearly he'd made certain rules and expected his daughters to keep them.

Three sets of stormy blue Walkington eyes fastened on her, each waiting for her to choose between them. "What do you think, Chastity?" Raven asked after a tense minute.

"She agrees with me," Lucas snapped. "Let's eat."

"I think..." Chastity said slowly, fighting to control the irritation that Lucas could easily arouse "...that we need to work on communication."

"'Communication.'"

"Lucas, stop repeating everything in one-word sentences."

He glanced at his daughters, who were watching the scene with interest. His expression changed to smothered, wary frustration. "Bet you can't sit in those tight jeans," he returned darkly. "Don't wear them outside the house."

"Sweetcakes..." Chastity began too softly, then remembered they were not alone. Because the girls were fascinated with the exchange, she decided that several matters would be resolved behind their bedroom door with Lucas's new lock. She sucked in her breath and pushed down the impulse to dump the roast, gravy, mashed potatoes and carrots over his head.

"Do the dishes. Then do your homework," Lucas ordered the girls immediately after dinner. He jerked on his hat and stalked out the door, slamming it behind him.

Raven threw a dish towel at the closed door. "I just might not want to go to college, Daddy."

The tears that Summer had been withholding throughout the meal began to drip into her plate.

Wayne howled softly from his safe cushion.

Chastity placed her hands flat on the table and studied the short, practical nails. Adept at smoothing family waters, she let her instincts take over. "Okay. He says dishes and homework."

Raven sniffed, wiping her sleeve across her eyes. "Daddy can be so grim."

"After dishes and homework, I say we party," Chastity continued with a bright grin, despite her breaking heart. The picture puzzle wasn't complete, but she saw Lucas struggling to hold on to everything he held dear, to manage as best he could. She ran her hand across her stomach. If his child rested there, Lucas would have another responsibility.

"Will you show us Hope's makeup tips?"

"Oh, my dah-lings," Chastity cooed. "She sent tons of makeup and perfume samples with me. There's nothing more relaxing than a good makeup session."

"Nails, too?" Raven asked and began stacking the dishes rapidly.

"My dears, we'll pedicure our hearts out. While we're at it, we'll plan an open-house party—"

Raven's grin died. "Daddy won't like the expense. He had to sell cattle for our Chicago fare."

The quiet statement slammed into Chastity's heart. Then Summer said, "Daddy said you were worth it. A good investment, he said. He said he'd mortgage the ranch to get you here."

Those words kept Chastity going full blast until Lucas settled into the bed beside her. He lay there stiffly in the moonlight, arms behind his head and staring at the ceiling. "The girls need their rest," he said in a tone resembling a bear inviting a fight. "The music was loud enough tonight to raise the dead."

"You should have joined us. The girls said you can dance."

Lucas snorted. "Self-protection. Had to learn to enter that Tulsa contest. They were on me like ticks on a dog."

Chastity sucked in her breath. Lucas could bend when necessary; it was a start. "We're having an open house here Friday night. You're cooking a pot of something. Maybe chili and make some of that jalapeño corn bread. The girls are making two chocolate cakes and—"

Lucas flipped onto her, covering her with his body. "You're taking over, are you, Miss Smarty-Pants?"

Because he was hurting, because he said she was worth mortgaging the ranch, Chastity gave him a respite from the pain. She gave him a nibbling kiss, massaged the taut muscles of his neck with her parted lips and wiggled beneath him. The distraction worked, and a short time later Lucas's kiss swallowed her soft scream of pleasure.

He levered his head down to her shoulder and fought to breathe evenly. "Primed...."

Nuzzling his hair and stroking his back, cherishing the way he'd given himself to her, Chastity hated to move. "Mmm."

"You are always primed, buttercup. Sweet and soft—"

Chastity shifted beneath him, holding him when he would have shifted aside. "Dear, I hope I didn't make too much noise."

Lucas's rich chuckle filled the room. "Scared the birds out of the trees outside."

"Goodness. Lucas, we've got to do something."

"Yep," he whispered hoarsely, moving deeply within her.

Then she laughed, holding him closer. He wanted her urgently and when she held him, stroking his hard shivering body until he slept, Chastity smiled in the darkness. Lucas Walkington would share more than his body with her, he would share his life.

* * *

"A man doesn't have to be social to love his daughters," Lucas snapped as he lifted Chastity up to the saddle. The Saturday after the Walkington's first Friday-night party was wonderful, filled with blue sky and Chastity ready for anything. Then the horse shifted and she screamed for Lucas, falling down into his arms.

He eased her back up into the saddle with a sharp, "Sit and hush up. You scream and Liz might run or buck."

"It's so far down to earth," Chastity whispered, gripping the saddle horn with both hands. Lucas swung up behind her and Chastity turned to wrap her arms around him. His legs tightened and the horse began to walk slowly.

His lips brushed her temple and stayed there, his arms strong and secure around her. "I managed to live through that party last night. You can manage this."

"Lucas, he's so wide! What if we fall?" she asked from beneath his chin.

"Liz is a she, Raven's horse. You won't be able to ride for long with the baby coming. Tell me what you learned about having a baby from the women Friday night." The horse walked slowly toward the grazing cattle.

"Uh...Lucas, I'll make an appointment with Dr. Blackwell in Muggins when I can find transportation. We've ridden enough, haven't we?" she asked hopefully. Liz stood near a cow, and Chastity clutched Lucas tighter. He probably wanted her to fall in a pit of cows to repay her for last night. She had worn the jeans, and when no one looked, Lucas's hand had smoothed her backside, a flush running beneath his dark skin, promising a long sensual night.

Lucas had taken her almost the minute the bedroom door closed that night. Of course he hadn't had a choice really. High on the party's success, she'd leaped on him, kissing him with all the joy in her. Duty-bound to respond, Lucas had answered the call magnificently.

"You wanted to ride," he said flatly. Then, "Transportation. Like the local transit system? I'll take you."

"The saddle is squeaking. Maybe you should oil it."

Lucas kissed her hard. "Oil that, buttercup. Stop talking. You rattle like a jaybird when you're scared."

"You're frightened, too. Your Code of the West, or almighty male rules, prevent you talking about it."

Lucas scowled down at her, his old Stetson shading his face. "That's bull—" Her set expression stopped him from finishing the word. "You're pushing, lady. Leave well enough alone."

"Leave well enough alone," Chastity repeated darkly after Lucas's pickup soared off into the night. The storm had been brewing all day. Raven and Summer stared at her, their young faces white beneath green mud masks. Chastity shook with anger that only Lucas had been able to raise. "Just where is he going at ten o'clock at night?"

"Maybe you shouldn't offer to help Daddy do the bills," Summer hesitantly suggested.

"Or ask what he's done about college preparation or looking into grants and aids," Raven added. "Telling him that not using coupons was like throwing away money could have riled him a little."

"Your father isn't an easy man, I'll admit that." Chastity inhaled, counted to ten and repeated her question, "Where is he going?"

"Mike's probably. It's a tavern in Chips. He hasn't been there for ages, but he's been looking like he wants to hole up."

"Hole up. Hide. From me. In a corner pub." Chastity was too angry to be hurt. "Help me pick out something to go with my new jeans, then take me to Mike's."

She paused, then said, "His hat never leaves his head unless he takes it off. Does the wind ever...or a limb...?"

"Daddy's hat never comes off unless he wants it off," Summer said flatly.

"Hmm." Just once, she promised, Lucas's hat would tumble away without his consent.

Nothing could have stopped her from dressing like Honey. She knew how to act like a barroom sweetie; once she had to track down a con man who had taken the Old Coot for a hundred dollars. She patted her flat stomach. "Daddy has a few rules to learn, sweetheart. If he wants to socialize, he can do it with us."

Lucas sipped his beer and sulked. He'd missed sulking since Chastity had arrived. A man deserved a real good sulk once in a while, especially since he'd found his brand-new wife could throw herself at him and every lick of horse sense he'd ever had sailed out into the night.

He stroked the cool perspiration on his beer mug thoughtfully. Chastity fascinated him, and if he were a kid he'd probably be in love with her. Soft and warm, she eased away the pain of his life. He'd have to gain some control or he'd fly apart when she left.

When she started talking about coupon savings and saving money, his pride had lurched. He'd wanted to take care of her, take her burdens; then suddenly she was exploring cost-saving ideas at the dinner table and riling him. He wanted to swathe her in care, keeping away the burdens she'd taken from her family.

Chastity deserved real parties, not put-together open houses with the neighbors pitching in casseroles and Jethro Ferguson's harmonica solo. Chastity's jeans had set him off, and he'd been in a froth from the moment he caught her body's sweet scent.

Chastity deserved more than part of a family ranch, a budget that didn't stretch and a man going nowhere fast.

A low wolf whistle and two catcalls brought Lucas's head up from his mug of beer. In the dark, smoky room filled with tables, chairs, a bar and a jukebox, a curvy blond woman with tight-fitting jeans walked toward him. The dim light traced a halo around a mass of curls that lay on her bare shoulders, then slipped down to touch the black knit top with long sleeves. The jeans hugged her waist and molded her hips and thighs, sliding down to her high-heeled boots.

She placed one of those high-heeled boots between his feet as he sprawled in a chair. "Hi, babe." Honey's sexy voice wrapped around him like a soft glove.

Lucas slashed an angry glance up at her as she sat on his knee. Every head in the tavern turned to them. Honey traced his lips with her tongue and her mouth slid into that mysterious, sloping smile.

"Hey, Lucas," Brad Koenig yelled. "Is that your wife?"

Honey waved airily, identifying herself. She draped her arm around Lucas's shoulder and waited, green eyes challenging him beneath her lashes. She ran a finger up his taut neck, scooped his hat off and placed it on her head.

Lucas wanted to sink into his sorrows, sulk and wallow, keeping the pain from his family. But there Honey sat, tilting his too-large hat back on her rippling, dark blond curls and surveying her new kingdom from his knee. He bounced that knee to jostle her and found himself meeting her grin. "You're ornery, woman," he muttered, suddenly happy and unwilling to show it.

"This is nice. I like this," she said, nodding as she looked at the various couples dancing and the usual byplay of single men and women. "The Old Coot, my grandfather, used to take me to places like this when I was little. He taught me how to play pool."

"Is that right?" Lucas had the feeling that no matter where his wife found herself, she could manage.

"Mmm. He felt sorry for me, I guess. Mother was so involved with Brent and Hope. Old Coot kept me so busy that I never missed being included...well, later, they needed me and things changed. He made me feel special, like I had secret talents all my own."

Pris Perkins eased her way to stand next to them. She moved the tray of empty glasses to her other hand and tugged down the tight, red satin blouse over her jeans. She skimmed Chastity's outfit, obviously comparing them mentally. Her glance at Lucas invited and challenged. "Does the lady want a drink, Luke?"

"Mineral water with lime, please," Chastity said, watching the other woman closely. Pris's painted eyes were hostile, her mouth tight beneath the glossy red-red lipstick. Unable to bear the thought of another woman in Lucas's arms, Chastity's fingers tightened almost painfully on Lucas's shoulder. "So, the first good tiff we have you run to one of your ex-loves, huh? That will have to stop, babe."

"Yes, ma'am," Lucas drawled, setting back to watch Chastity. She fascinated him, a creature who moved between people and worlds and sensed pain, probing it out with soft, delicate fingers, then stroking the wounds until they eased.

Chastity's fingers drummed his shoulder, her lips tightening. "Yes, I suppose that what's in the past is done. You would have had relationships...." She chewed on that, glanced at the jukebox and stood, tugging him to stand. "Let's dance, babe. You've done enough sulking."

Lucas lay tangled with his sleeping wife hours later and wondered what hit him.

Wiggling up and over him, Chastity yawned. "I've never made love in a sleeping bag before, sweetcakes. We're lucky you had one in the pickup."

He stroked her hair, savoring the fresh clean scent that blended with the smells of the earth and new grass. "Your experience is limited."

Kissing one side of his mouth, then the other, Chastity tugged his hair. "You should know." Then, for a long time, Lucas's world was soft and sweet, easing away the years of strain.

Chastity rubbed her cheek against his chest. "Babe, I'm ready to listen."

Lucas caught her head, held her lips against him, her body tight. In a matter of days, they would know about the baby. Whatever happened, he didn't want to let Chastity leave him.

"I'm not going anywhere, Lucas," she whispered, stroking his shoulder.

"The Walkington land was once four hundred acres," Lucas began slowly, nuzzling the fragrant curls that drifted around him on the midnight breeze. His arms tightened around her, keeping her close to soothe the pain. "My great-grandparents claimed it in the land run on Oklahoma territory. My grandparents added to it, and my folks died holding hands in a blizzard while I was off sowing wild oats. The sod house my great-great-grandparents built was on the land I sold when I was twenty-one and trying to impress Alesha. It seemed right back then. I couldn't handle the stock, the land or a high-priced girl who wanted to play."

He closed his eyes, the tear trail cold on his temples. "Someone should have put me out of my misery. When I dropped off the roller coaster we were on, two hundred acres were gone, oil rigs bobbing up and down on the old Walkington spread. By the time I came to my senses, Alesha was pregnant."

Chastity's hand was soft against his cheek. "You were young, Lucas. You can't blame yourself for eternity."

"I didn't buy much with the money, but hard times. Most of it's gone now and my daughters' heritage with it.... Hard thing for a man to swallow...that he had sold away his family's future."

"Oh, sweetheart, you were young."

Lucas swallowed, his throat hurting with emotion. He hadn't shared the pain, and now he found himself trembling. "The water went with the land. We're on the dry side. In the summer I haul water for the cattle."

"Shh." Her fingertip sealed his lips and Lucas kissed it. "Everything will be just fine."

"Uh-huh," he tossed back, disbelieving. "Sure."

"One thing at a time, Lucas-babe," Chastity murmured, moving over him.

He remembered laughing before the tropical storm took him.

Eight

The moment Lucas placed Chastity on her feet behind their bedroom door, he started unbuttoning her blouse. He hadn't said an entire sentence on their way home from the doctor in Muggins, and Chastity fought her tears. She wanted him to do all those fabulous, endearing things expectant fathers did, but not her babe.

The bright April morning sunshine shot through the windows and Wayne whined beyond the closed door. Lucas tipped back his hat and unbuttoned the front of her skirt, almost tearing the fabric.

"Well," she exclaimed in a soft whoosh as he tugged her slip, panty hose and briefs to her ankles. Bracing her hand on his shoulder as he jerked her undergarments off and tossed the bundle into a chair, Chastity drummed her fingers on the solid muscle. "Well," she said again when he stripped off her bra. "This is nice. Yes. Very nice indeed. Classy. Cowboy learns for certain that he's going to be a father again after many years. Cowboy takes wife home and strips her."

Chastity crossed her arms across a swelling bosom that Lucas bent to study intently. "It's all the same basic equipment you married," she said between her teeth as his open hand skimmed down her stomach, flattening over it.

"Hush," he ordered gently, turning her around to study her backside. Two big hands slid down her ribs to her hips, his thumbs stretching to touch in the center. Then turning her slowly again, Lucas lifted her hair back from her throat and pried her arms away.

"This isn't quite how I thought you'd react, babe," she muttered as he traced her jawbone, sliding his hands down to cup her breasts. He concentrated on the rounded weight, lightly running his fingers across her sensitive nipples.

"Mmm?" he asked in a distant tone, continuing to study her stomach, probing it gently with his thumbs.

"Sweetcakes, you don't act extremely happy," Chastity said evenly, despite the anger and fear raging inside her.

To balance her simmering emotions, she tossed at him, "Do you know that your hat always stays on until you take it off? I mean the wind never moves it. It never falls off. That can be very irritating at times."

When she had cornered him in a stall, the hat had tilted awry as they made love, but remained in place.

"Stetson," he returned in a distracted tone, as if the brand name explained everything.

"Oh."

Lucas flattened both hands low on her stomach, frowning. "Babies kick at four and a half to five months, the doctor said.... You're just six weeks along— It's real then," he whispered huskily, lifting his eyes to hers.

She loosened her fists. One more minute of Lucas's grim treatment, and she was prepared to hit the nearest dimple. Not that he'd been showing them lately.

The wonder and excitement she'd wanted shimmered in the tears shining in Lucas's dark blue eyes. Every dram of the sweet new father expression swirled around Lucas's face, lifting his mouth in a silly, boyish, dimple-creasing grin. He spanned her waist with shaking, callused hands. "It's true. I was afraid.... A baby. It's going to kick, right there in your soft little belly."

Chastity began to smile, then Lucas's face paled. "I . . . I feel weak." Before she could grab him, he sprawled backward on the bed.

"Lucas!" As she bent over him, Lucas snared her hand weakly.

"Where are the girls?" His voice was weak, and a fine perspiration glowed on his forehead.

"In school. They'll be home in a few hours." Badly frightened, Chastity leaned over him to place her hand on his cold, damp forehead. She smoothed a thick wave back from his brow. "What's wrong, sweetheart?"

"Let me lay here a minute. I'm winded, that's all. Don't let the girls see me like this," he rasped unevenly, then closed his eyes. His lashes lay black and lush against his paling complexion.

"Lucas, you're scaring the daylights out of me! Wake up!" Chastity slapped him hard, trying to remember where the emergency telephone numbers were located.

"Hey! Lay off," Lucas mumbled, rubbing his damaged cheek. She noted that like that of a true cowboy, Lucas's hat had remained on his head. His fall had merely tilted the angle.

His grin was devastating, all tanned angles and dimples and shining blue eyes with black lashes. The room's filtered sunlight bounced off his teeth in a blinding ray. Chastity jerked his belt buckle upward hard. "You low-down yahoo. You're scaring me to death."

"Must have had too much sun.... You, Mrs. Walkington, are one-hundred-percent certified pregnant with my baby."

"Of course I am. That's no reason to faint. Lucas, you need a doctor."

He drew her palm to his lips and kissed it. "I didn't faint. Just feeling a little tired. Ever slap a man before?"

The delicate nibbling around her palm excited and soothed. "I've never had reason to, Lucas."

He tugged her down beside him, laying on his side to study her. Running his thumb along her jawbone, he noted, "You've gotten a little rounder here."

His hand opened, running along her throat and down to cup her breast. "Why did you slap me, buttercup?"

"I once had to save Brent from a mean, muscular bill collector. We faked his fainting spell to get Brent to safety. I had to slap him quite hard to make it believable."

"So I got the slap of experience, right?"

Chastity snuggled up to him, slipping her hand inside his dress shirt to stroke his broad chest. "Only because I care, babe. Now tell me why you acted like Granite Man at the doctor's."

The seconds stretched into her heart, making it ache. She'd wait until forever to understand his pain. Lucas studied the shafts of afternoon light crossing into the room, his lashes catching it in blue-black tints. "After Alesha found out she was pregnant, we never made love again. Had the devil's own time persuading her to keep the babies. When she found out she carried twins, all hell broke loose."

He turned slowly to her, his expression tight with pain. "She was gone to her folks more than not. Wouldn't let me touch her, or see the changes in her body. I couldn't live with a woman carrying my baby and not share the experiences as it became real." The grim lines settled around Lucas's mouth.

Chastity removed his hat and tossed it to a bedpost. "Learned that from one of mother's beaux." She pushed her fingers through Lucas's hair, letting the texture and warmth slip along her skin. "I'm not Alesha. You're sweet, Lucas."

He snorted at that. "The hell you say. When we made love that first time, I gave a part of myself to you. That's why I pushed so hard to get you back here with me. There's not much here, but what there is belongs to my children, all of them." He rubbed her stomach, bending to kiss it.

Her fingers tightened in his hair, keeping him near, and Lucas lifted his eyes questioningly. She wanted to tell him she loved him, to ask if he might care, but the dark blue eyes were heating, flowing over her breasts hungrily. Could he love her? Could he tuck his first experience at love in a drawer and open his heart? "Lucas...I..."

He kissed her stomach again lower and Chastity sucked in her breath, tensing.

The third kiss sent her into trembling shudders while Lucas watched intently. When she blushed, he chuckled. "Sweet bit, maybe we'd better start taking walks after supper. The doctor said to exercise...." The wicked look in his eyes deepened her blush.

"Wicked man," Chastity mumbled at seven the next morning, long after Lucas had gone out to check on the cattle. Later he would help Orvy Holiday lay bricks and pour concrete for an addition to his house.

While Lucas worked and the girls were at school, the echo of her soft scream had clung to her for hours. High and quivering it had swept through the damp night air hovering over the meadow, startling her. She glanced darkly at Wayne who sat amid piles of papers near the bedroom desk. Chastity balled another scrap of paper and tossed it at him, which he dutifully caught in his teeth and placed in a growing pile of wadded balls.

She jotted a number on a column in Raven's discarded notebook. "I am to rest. I am to put my little feet up, take vitamins and rest. I am not a partner in this marriage. *I am a love-toy for a babe*. A cowboy whose hat never, ever tips or tilts or leaves his head unless he wishes. *He* makes decisions for me, just as though I was one of the twins. *He* says..." she lowered her voice in mock male tones "...'Stay in the house, take your itty-bitty nap while I fight the world and take the bruises on my big wide cowboy shoulders.' ''

Had she told him she loved him in the night's passionate heat?

Wayne, a good listener, tilted his head and flopped to his feet with a snort. Chastity continued to sort, file, and jot figures into the notebook. Lucas's bookkeeping consisted of his mysterious notes, a drawer of canceled checks and an assortment of coupons from magazines, clearly clipped by young girls wanting cosmetics, body waves and perfumes. Chastity checked the expiration dates on the coupons, sorted them into neatly marked envelopes and addressed an envelope for a rebate ticket. Stacking Lucas's farm, seed and cattle magazines neatly, she carried them to the kitchen and began clipping coupons and rebates.

By the time Melody arrived, without her children, to share morning coffee, Chastity was picking through cereal boxes and peeling labels off detergent bottles for coupons. "I've never gotten into that, but they say you can save a lot if you work at it."

Chastity blew back a curl and snipped around a discount coupon for men's jeans. She'd been couponing since Old Coot bought her a special pair of non-sharp children's scissors. Until his last years in the nursing home, the Old Coot was the guardian of the coupons, a task she had inherited with his talent. Necessary to balance her mother's poor management, the coupons provided everything. As a child, Chastity accompanied the Old Coot to various waiting rooms with the sole purpose of snipping coupons. A child went unnoticed, and the task occupied her for an hour or so until Old Coot delegated another waiting room. She spent many hours happily clipping the coupons that the Old Coot had stealthily noted. "The trick is in organizing. I'm sending off for an organizer that comes with this coupon for soap."

"Mmm...what does Lucas think about coupons?" Melody asked cautiously over the rim of her cup.

"They're great. What else would he think?"

"That man has too much pride. He needed help watering stock a few years ago. The only way he'd take help was if he could pay them back. When he lost that hay crop two years ago and the girls had complications from the flu, we thought he would kill himself working to pay everyone back. He did look real cute behind John's counter measuring out laces and ribbons. He's stiff-backed, Honey. You might work up to the subject and see what he thinks, before you act."

"Rubbish. Coupons are an American right," Chastity quoted Old Coot.

"You might ask, just the same. Lucas might consider it some kind of charity." Then Melody went on about her children and marveled at Chastity's plants. Encompassing an entire corner, they would be moved to the porch in warmer weather. The new friends spent the next hour visiting over seed catalogs, which Chastity thought was a marvelous Oklahoma right.

Longing for a garden, Chastity asked the younger woman's advice, and together they walked around the new garden plot. "It needs volunteer plants like garlic and winter onions. Maybe sage... There are things that come up every year. How about a ladies' coffee some morning, and I'll ask everyone to bring a plant or something for the garden? Maybe some berry starts and daffodils. That old elderberry bush down by Lucas's windmill always has berries. You need water for other berries, Honey, and this land is dry. In the summer, we use every barrel, every kiddie pool, to hold water for our gardens."

She grinned widely. "You'll have a pool in the yard, just like everyone else before long."

Chastity returned the grin, running her hand down her stomach. "I just can't believe it. The baby is such a long time away. Nothing seems real yet."

"Better enjoy it. Lucas is walking on air, but he needs to stop working so hard." Melody shrugged, running her hand down her rounded tummy. "Doctor and hospital bills are high. Marlene Kleinhoffer is a great midwife, has been for years. She'd love to work with you and whatever doctor you're using."

"Lots of neighborhoods in Chicago have them. I'd love that."

Chastity spent the afternoon alternately coveting seed catalogs with fruit trees and berries and developing a clear picture of Lucas's finances. He paid cash, tossed receipts into boxes, wrote few checks on a small account and contributed irregular deposits to the twins' savings.

Tapping a pencil on her bottom lip, Chastity walked around the house and thought deeply about her relationship with Lucas. He kept his fears neatly tucked away, growled at those who came too close and was frustrated by the growing breach between him and the twins. Clearly Lucas was deeply tired, physically—well, not always, she allowed—and mentally. The baby and herself would be added expenses if he were to have his way.

Chastity frowned and adjusted her glasses. She had never been anyone's excess baggage and she wouldn't let Lucas take that away from her. No babe was going to stand in his well-fixed jeans and— She inhaled slowly, forcing her anger away, and thinking logically as the Old Coot had taught her to do when planning scams. She, Lucas, the girls and the baby were a family and a family shared responsibilities. She would not live on the borders of another family as she had in Chicago, existing when they chose to recognize her.

"Daddy won't like it," Raven said firmly, hours later.

"Daddy hasn't had time to go to school. There are financial aids and grants available for us. We brought home the forms, but he seems to think college is a cash basis only. The other kids' parents went to the advisor and worked with him. There's stuff available if you send off for it," Summer added. "But Daddy is always tired and we—we argued a lot before you came. We want to date, Chastity, and Daddy is acting like an old—"

"Fuddy-duddy?" Chastity supplied, and grinning. "He's not at all. He loves you and he wants the best for you." She suspected Lucas's fears ran to seeing the girls make his youthful mistakes.

Over sandwiches drinks, and clipping coupons the girls chattered about school events and the special boys they wanted to date. The boys were interested, but Lucas stood between young love like an enraged, battle-wise sheepdog tending lambs. Later, as they showed Chastity how to milk a cow, they talked about clothes and how they wanted to dress. "Clothes shouldn't be a problem," Chastity said, concentrating on a plump, milk-filled udder.

"Jeans are practical. There are skirts and blouses, too. Mother took us shopping, but we left those things at her house. They weren't our style, anyway. Daddy would know how much brand-name clothing costs and it might . . . well, hurt him."

Chastity tried to avoid the cow's swishing tail. "What about thrift shops or garage sales? I always loved the things from used clothing stores. They didn't cost that much and you could make them over to be just great. I worked at a dry cleaner's after school for an entire year and learned how to tailor." She omitted the family obsession with stylish clothes and how she had altered endlessly.

"There's a used clothing store in Muggins," Raven ventured. "But won't people recognize their own throwaways?"

"Nope. Not after refashioning and dyeing. Why does that calf keep mooing?"

"That's Lacy's calf. She has plenty of milk, but Angel doesn't want to share." Summer lifted the bucket, scanning it. "Dad gives the cream to Mrs. Nelson for butter. She took care of us last year when we had the flu. Daddy worked right through his flu."

Chastity stood and rubbed her hands on her thighs, scanning the calves playing in the fields. Her babe, her sweetcakes, had a mountain to learn about sharing and giving and relationships and loving.

As if on cue, Raven warned, "Daddy won't like you organizing his business desk. He likes to keep that stuff to himself."

"Not anymore," Chastity promised flatly.

At ten o'clock that night, Lucas's pickup stopped in front of the house. Wayne barked frantically, wagging his tail, and barreled out of the door the minute Chastity opened it. Lucas entered the house, his hat dusty, his jeans and workman's boots gray with concrete dust. Carrying Wayne on his hip, he sighed, slid a one-dimple smile in her direction and opened the refrigerator door, scanning the contents.

When he tipped back his hat, the appliance's light spread across his face. Beneath the dirt, lines of fatigue ran deep.

"Hi, Daddy." Raven and Summer looked up from stacks of clothing, the old portable sewing machine reigned over a jumble of thread and cloth on the kitchen table.

Chastity stood in the shadows and ached. Barely standing upright, Lucas eased Wayne to the floor and patted the dog's curly head. Then he found her in the shadows and his eyes lit up. "Hi, Mrs. Walkington," he said in that low, intimate twang.

"Hi, babe," she returned, her stomach contracting painfully, while her heart raced as the dark blue eyes slid over her.

Lucas's gaze seemed to inhale every inch of her body beneath his oversize shirt. "Come here."

The gentle command spoke of hunger and need, and Chastity could not refuse. Standing in front of him, she lifted her lips and kissed him with all her heart amid the twins' catcalls. When the kiss was finished, Lucas closed his eyes and leaned his forehead against hers.

Vulnerable and weary, he nuzzled her cheek and Chastity wrapped her arms around him tightly. "I missed you, babe," she whispered against his lips and nibbled at them until she felt the tug of his lazy smile.

She rubbed her hand across his back and Lucas sighed, his body rippling beneath her touch like a big cat being petted. "If you shower, I'll fix dinner."

"I meant to start stew this morning, but had other things on my mind," he whispered huskily. "You shouldn't be cooking. You should be resting."

She grinned while Lucas showered. No matter how tired that Oklahoma babe was, he always made her feel desirable. He grumbled at the dinner she had warmed, a mock beef Stroganoff with noodles, and ate half the coffee cake she had baked that morning. While he was grumbling and managing a conversation with the girls about schoolwork, Lucas rubbed Wayne's belly with his toes. He toyed with her fingers as he ate and finished his iced tea, the area's standard beverage. In a weary voice Lucas informed her that before dawn, he would rise to help Sam Ledbetter fertilize a south pasture and repair fence.

He looked so tired and sweet, she didn't have the heart to tell him that coupons, financial aids and grants, and boyfriends for his daughters lurked in his future. Or that she had organized his desk and the twins and herself were shopping at the Muggins used clothing store next Saturday. Or that John's grocery, feed and grain had acquired an at-home, Johnny-come-lately Chicago-bred bookkeeper.

Or that she loved him very much.

"What the hell happened to my desk? Where are my papers?" Lucas's indignant roar shook the bedroom before dawn. He ripped open the scarred desk's drawers, glared at the neat arrangements and opened a shoe box filled with alphabetical envelopes that were stuffed with clipped coupons. "What is this?" he asked between his teeth, thumbing through the coupons.

Struggling up from the tangled bedding, clinging to Lucas's pillow and keeping his scent close at hand, Chastity blew away the curls from her face that he had nuzzled sweetly throughout the night. She struggled with the sweet tingles Lucas had created with his lovemaking sometime during the night and the scowling cowboy glaring down at her.

Legs spread wide, his jeans unsnapped and his shirt unbuttoned, Lucas didn't look sweet and vulnerable. Not at all the man who had held her as if she were a part of him, not the vulnerable man who had let her comfort him with caresses and soft kisses. She cleared her throat, pasting an innocent baby-doll expression on her face, and wished that she had told him everything last night.

"Now, sweetcakes. The girls are still sleeping." She smiled the Honey smile à la Hope's instructions.

"I can understand the sewing mess and the girls wanting to show you off at school and meet their teachers. I can understand chaperoning the school prom two weeks away. Females are likely to be in cahoots. I expected that from the start. Women make nests. There's female bonding and such . . . but, by God, you will leave my desk alone!"

Chastity shifted on the bed, covered her bare shoulder with a blanket and couldn't keep the baby-doll smile from slipping. She bit her lower lip to keep it from trembling. Lucas sat on the bed, jammed his feet into socks and never let his sizzling blue stare leave her face.

His silent challenge was too much. "You needed help," Chastity explained. "Organization. I'm a bookkeeper and—"

"Git." Wayne's wagging stub of a tail stopped and he slunk into the living room.

"Be reasonable, Lucas—" Chastity began when Lucas stood and began buttoning his shirt in angry, jerking movements. "I'm only two months' pregnant. I've been an active, useful person my entire life. You can't expect me to live off you without—"

"I take care of my family, lady. Since you snooped, you probably know just how little we have."

"I've lived on the outside of one family, Lucas," Chastity shot back, aware that no one but her babe and sweetcakes had the ability to draw anger out of her like wildfire igniting tinder. "I will not be less than I am with my own husband, low-down macho cowboy, dimpled cheeks and devastating charm, ornery as you are, Lucas Walkington. Your finances are my finances and they're not that bad. A little reorganization can help you save time and money. Using coupons and investing the girls' savings accounts into better-earning interest accounts is a simple matter."

He grabbed the Stetson, plopped it on the back of his head and stared at her.

"Don't try to frighten me like you do your daughters, babe," Chastity said grimly.

"You messed up my desk." The quiet accusation was a roar of anger and indignation.

"Organization. Files. I'm good at that." She omitted the singular talent the Old Coot had bestowed upon her. If Lucas couldn't digest organization, he certainly wasn't ready for a water witch. Of course she had brushing up to do before trying her abilities. Lately forks had been quivering in her hand when she concentrated on the dripping faucet and...

"Lady, you are to rest and let me take care of you," Lucas began heavily.

"I have been taking care of myself for years, Mr. Walkington. I have capabilities and talents you haven't even guessed," she tossed back, jerking on his T-shirt, which had been tossed aside during their tender lovemaking.

"Uh-huh. Troublemaking and what else?"

The challenge was too much and Chastity hit him with a pillow, lunging for him and taking him down to the bed. She climbed over him and held his wrists to the pillow like a wrestler pinning an opponent. When he grinned, pulling out the dimples, she realized that he had fallen too easily. The words she had been holding sailed out into the pink dawn beyond their room. "I'm clipping coupons, managing *our* records, working as John's part-time bookkeeper, growing my garden and loving you."

She hadn't noticed Lucas's body tensing beneath her, the sudden, dazed surprise in his expression, nor the way his fingers had curled around hers. She took a deep breath and released her untried secret into the sweet, morning air. "Lucas, I am a water witch."

"You love me," he repeated unevenly, his expression stunned as he ignored the admission of her lifelong secret.

"Of course. True, you're not a logical choice. Entirely too proud. But I do and that's that." Chastity blew a bobbing curl away from her left eye. She hoped she hadn't frightened him with her water witch admission. Any minute he would suggest therapy. She could tell by the sweet, dazed, confused expression on his bearded face.

The telephone by the bed rang and Lucas reached for it, at the same time jamming a pillow behind his back. His gaze ran over her face and Chastity inhaled sharply. Learning that one's wife was a water witch—true, an untried water witch—could be a shattering experience for the poor dear. A sinking-ship feeling centered in her chest and slid slowly to the pit of her stomach. She swallowed as he frowned, listening to the caller. "She's right here."

Placed at a time when she was most vulnerable, the call was from her mother. Chattering about Brent's love affairs and bill collectors and Hope's quest for Lyle, because his wife didn't understand him, nor his three children, Grace took a breath and asked, "How are you, precious?"

"Precious" was hauled on her new husband's lap and being cuddled and being kissed sweetly. No doubt Lucas wanted to calm her before suggesting an analyst. While she tried to concentrate on her mother's delicate pleas for help in managing another credit card fiasco, Chastity focused on Lucas's dimples.

He nibbled on her earlobe and whispered, "You tell her she can go to—"

"What?" Grace squawked while Lucas nibbled his way to Chastity's throat. "Is Lucas saying something, dear?"

Chastity tried to concentrate. The task was difficult. Lucas was unwrapping her from blankets and sheets as though she were his special birthday gift. Poor dear, he hadn't realized that she wasn't lean and leggy yet. "We'll go the coupon route and you can file to your little heart's content," he whispered, studying her body in the morning shadows, his expression filled with wonder as his thumb traced her hipbone.

Her heart quivered, pounding rapidly. Tender and vulnerable, Lucas placed his dark hand across her stomach, moving it gently around the smooth contour.

"Mother, buy a calculator," Chastity said huskily, enchanted by Lucas's expression of awe. "I'll write you when we're more settled. Oklahoma is wonderful—yes, I said get a calculator. Hope can balance your checkbook. Check the expiration date on the coupons. Bye."

Nine

Chastity inhaled the clear May air and wiggled her bare toes in the dirt of her Oklahoma garden. She pushed Brent's plea—rescue from an adoring redhead whom he had promised to marry—into the clear blue sky. Her mother's voluminous package of overdue bills and various notices from credit-card companies rested in the Walkington's rural mailbox. Chastity had returned the packaged clutter with a simple note: "Mother, do not charge anything. Ask Hope or Brent to help you."

Then, because she loved her family, she'd managed to add, "You're a woman of courage. You couldn't have raised the three of us and managed Old Coot without a talent for balancing figures. A little patience and practice and you'll be fine. Tell Hope and Brent that I'm fine and I love you all."

She frowned at a tiny weed invading her precious piece of Oklahoma and bent to pluck it from her carefully planned rows of green beans. The garden was small, a delight to manage. Sage, garlic and winter onions nestled against an old picket fence that had stood in Lucas's great-grandmother's time. Wayne basked in the sun, annoyed by the calves he was not allowed to chase. He growled at the cattle, demonstrating his poodle ferocity. His nails gleamed with Summer's new Adorable Pink polish.

Chastity tenderly smoothed Lucas's worn shirt over her stomach, then hugged herself, keeping him close.

The Walkingtons were facing each other like dogs over a bone. The girls wanted to date, wanted all that they deserved as young women meeting life's trials. Lucas wanted to protect them from bruises. While the Walkingtons' love ran deep, a frontier showdown could occur if the matter weren't resolved and soon.

Construction of a new gym had begun, and Lucas had taken a job as a workman. Tired and snappy, he checked the stock before dawn, left for work and returned at nightfall, barely able to shower and fall into bed. The temporary job paid well, and Chastity sensed Lucas's desperation to provide for his family.

She'd watched him stare at the rise separating his ranch from the old one. At those times, his pain swirled around him like a dark, aching cloak, his expression grim.

The old windmill caught the wind, clacking away with three missing blades. The budding elderberry bush shimmered in the sun. Chastity stepped from her garden and wiggled her toes on the hard-packed earth. ''It's a good scam, Old Coot. I'm just where I want to be. Though Lucas-babe is one tough nut to crack. He has far too much pride, and I suspect he is deeply afraid of losing this last part of his heritage.''

Lucas's lovemaking was contained, gentle and beautiful. She wanted the desperation, the intensity and the flame of his desire before the doctor's examination.

The wind riffled through the elderberry bush and Chastity stroked the baby who lay cradled in her womb. Lucas had given her his child and he would give her more—a life filled with happiness and love.

That night Lucas walked into the house, slammed the door behind him and ordered Wayne to "git."

Raven and Summer slid wary looks at Chastity, who took a deep breath and launched herself at him. She managed to tilt his dusty hat, the force of her body taking him back against the wall. While he tried to avoid her tiny kisses, she persisted and received a one-dimple smile. His hand stroked her back gently. "I hear the Walkington females have been busy."

The drawl sounded like a warning growl of a cornered wolf. One who wanted to fight.

Chastity patted his dimple, meeting his stormy blue stare innocently. "Things to do, people to see."

"John Blue Sky has a brand-new, nifty, bona fide Chicago bookkeeper. Says she works part-time, building credit on her account."

"That's me, Lucas. I told you I had taken a job—"

He swept that bit of information away like a clinging straw. "There you stand, barefoot and pregnant and *working when you shouldn't be.*" Lucas's indignant tone raised Chastity's hackles.

She smiled, wiggled her bare toes against the cool linoleum and forced the corners of her mouth to lift equally. "I'm used to working, Lucas. The girls pick up the invoices and cash tickets on their way home from school and deliver my work in the morning. It's a few hours spent punching a calculator on the kitchen table. I'm capable and there's no reason on earth why I shouldn't be working now."

Lucas's jaw, dusted with concrete and rough with a day's stubble, locked in place. "There's me. I say you take it easy." He glanced at the girls lying on the floor and watching television. "While we're on the subject, who is doing all the cooking around here? Raven, Summer, you will not let—"

Both girls rose to their feet. The tall Walkingtons glared at each other over Chastity's head. "Honey likes to cook, Dad," Raven said tightly.

"We like casseroles and pasta dishes, Dad. When her spinach comes in, we're having salad from it," Summer added.

"Uh-huh," Lucas returned in the same tone, unimpressed with Chastity's fresh spinach salad. "I'm going out to the barn. Summer, fold those towels I washed this morning."

"I folded them, Lucas," Chastity said quietly.

His blue eyes sliced down to her with the hardness of steel. "You are to rest, lady, and quit that damn job!"

"You're cheating Honey, Dad," Summer stated flatly, tears brimming to her eyes. "She's a modern woman, just like *we* want to be."

"She knows things that could help and—" Raven stopped when Lucas shot her a hard stare. She inhaled sharply, clutched her school notebook in her hand and said, "Dad, if anyone is doing wrong by Honey, it's you—"

The whirlwind discussion slashed over Chastity's head and she fought for a way to smother it gently.

"Wrong by me? What do you mean?" Lucas ripped off his leather gloves and tossed them on the counter, glaring down at Chastity.

Wayne whined and Chastity's heart thudded in the stark silence. "Ah...dinner is waiting. It's a lovely tuna casserole." Chastity hoped that the tension would settle over her special tuna-noodle bake. Emily Newcomer's homegrown tarragon sprigs rested in her new batch of vinegar—

"Honey is talented, Dad," Raven stated flatly. "She's a modern woman who rises to her challenges, just like we could be...*if you ever let us start dating.*"

Summer stood stiffly, tears dripping from her cheeks. "Dad, you've got to let us be us. Everything isn't always money and hard work, there's more...and if you don't stop acting like an old bear, you're going to lose Honey," she wailed, jumping over a stack of clothes and running into her room.

Raven straightened her shoulders, looked straight at Lucas, sniffed once and followed her sister, walking very straight. Lucas stared at the twins' closed bedroom door, his expression taut. He swallowed, ran his hand over his stubbled jaw, blinked and asked, "What happened?"

Chastity decided that the matter of shopping at Muggins's thrift shop could wait. She gripped her hands tightly. "I'm afraid I said we needed to express ourselves more...to work on our relationships—"

"Relationships? Communicate?" Lucas slashed at her. "Lady, I can communicate. *What I say goes.*"

The lordly tone settled on Chastity like spiny thistles on silk. She smiled tightly. "Is that so, Mr. Lucas-babe Walkington?"

"Are you checking out?" he snapped back. "Getting too rough for you?"

She tapped her toe. "Lucas, please don't make me lose my temper."

"Fine," he returned impatiently. "Look, this is the way it is. You need to rest—"

"I am so tired of that phrase, Lucas-babe," Chastity cautioned. "And the last time I rested, I found myself being stampeded into Oklahoma. I'm awake now and you have got to stop ordering me around." Her soft tone rose, the quiet yell infuriating her. Only Lucas could make her lose control, and she resented it.

"They are too young to date," he snapped doggedly, ignoring his campaign to lasso her.

"If they don't date here, Lucas, they will away from home. It might be wiser if you let them try their dating wings while living at home."

Lucas shot her a look of enraged fear. "You seemed happy enough. I thought puttering in that garden made you happy. Are you leaving me?"

She ached for him, the rigid pain digging into the lines on his face. His fists clenched at his thighs.

"You need me, Lucas, to keep you from getting old and set in your ways," she whispered softly, then stood on tiptoe to kiss his tight lips. She nibbled a bit at the hard contours until they softened slightly.

"Everything happened so fast," he whispered huskily, his hands smoothing her waist. "First they were little tadpoles and now..." The helpless tone slid inside her heart, causing it to ache.

Sliding her arms around him, Chastity held him tightly. "Everything will be just fine, Lucas-babe. Would you take a walk with me?"

The bedroom door jerked open. "Can we have dates for the prom, Dad?" Raven and Summer asked at the same time.

Chastity cuddled closer. "Say 'yep,' babe."

Lucas adjusted his tie, then jerked it loose while he watched his daughters dance in the boys' arms. "They're plastering themselves against my little girls," he muttered darkly as Chastity slipped into his arms to dance. He continued watching the twins over her head, his jaw moving as he ground his teeth. "Pimply, skinny things with *their hands on my girls' waists.*"

Chastity jerked him closer. "Raven and Summer want to date those pimply things."

His eyebrows shot up. "That Brewer kid and the Jones boy? I remember when they were born. That Brewer kid got stuck in a pipe when he was four and I had to haul him out. That Jones boy has never had a lick of horse sense."

"What do you think about the girls' dresses?"

Lucas continued to stare at the boys dancing with his daughters. "Told them to get one out of the catalog and charge it."

"You made them feel wonderful tonight, Lucas, when they were all dressed. They were proud of you, too," she began, wanting to tell him that the dresses would not appear on his charge card. "You were gallant, making them feel like princesses."

"They're my little girls. Scared me to see them all fixed up like grown women. Damn . . . look at that . . ."

Just then Mel Jones's cheek pressed against Raven's, and Chastity had to grip Lucas's belt to keep him against her. The time was not ripe to tell him that Raven and Summer wore gowns, purchased on discount and refashioned with satin and lace found in the bottom of a thrift-store box. The pink sequins splashing the gowns were pirated from Honey's dress.

Later, Lucas jerked the curtain away from the window and peered into the night. "It's late. Where are they?"

Chastity leaned against him, rubbing his taut rear end affectionately. "There's a breakfast at the Brewer's house after the prom."

"Stop that." Lucas pressed his hand over her roaming one as it slid inside his jeans.

"I'm proud of you, sweetcakes," Chastity whispered, cuddling against his broad back. "You only shot a glare or two when the four of them left."

"Those Brewer and Jones boys have been away at college for a year. No telling what they've learned."

Chastity nuzzled his muscled arm, loving to comfort him. "You're the one with growing pains."

"All this goes against the grain. They won't need me at all before long," Lucas muttered.

"They'll always need you and so will I," Chastity whispered against his mouth. "Come let me show you how much."

The first week of June, Lucas slapped his severance paycheck against his dusty jeans and settled back into the pickup seat to overlook the starry night. The construction had swung into another phase and the company used its own men to finish the building. All local work force was given a thank-you-very-much and a fat severance check.

"Lucas, your middle name is hard times," he muttered. With dry weather at his doorstep, a pregnant wife and looming doctor bills, his daughters needing dental care, he was out of work.

He'd swept Chastity from her safe job, her relatives, into another pit of needs.

Dreams really didn't last. He started the pickup, jammed it into gear and drove slowly into the ranch yard.

He managed to eat Chastity's pasta salad despite the hard lump in his stomach. The weed lurking in her special vinegar didn't make the spinach salad taste better. The twins' stories of boys, clothes, and cars slid off him like rainwater. When dinner was finished, Lucas sipped his iced tea, stroked his thumb over the beads of moisture on his glass and said, "I lost my job."

He explained briefly about the company using its own crews and petted Wayne, who had hopped up on his lap.

Chastity gripped her fork, which was shaking violently in the direction of the dripping water faucet. She placed it carefully on the table and reached for Lucas's hand. The twins avoided looking at him, waiting for the worst.

"Lucas, don't worry so. This would be a perfect time for you to enclose the porch for another room."

"Money, Chastity. Boards and nails cost. Feed costs, gas and food—"

"My garden is doing beautifully. We've got time to enlarge it. I've always wanted to preserve food. It's much more healthy."

"Water, Chastity. A large garden takes plenty of water. Then there's the baby—"

Raven lifted her head. Fear quivered in her voice as she said, "You're not selling Rosebud."

"Of course, he's not. Rosebud is too precious," Chastity said as Lucas took a deep breath. "He hasn't even thought of selling your calf, Raven."

"He's selling Rosebud," Raven said flatly. Then, when Lucas did not deny it, she jumped up and ran to her bedroom.

"Not Rosebud," Summer said quietly before following her sister.

"That heifer will bring good money at an auction," Lucas said doggedly when Chastity turned to him.

"Lucas, surely there's another way...."

"Not likely. Lady, you married a loser," Lucas bit out as he stood, reaching for his hat. Then Chastity was at the door, holding her arms across her chest, blocking him from licking his wounds alone.

"You haven't discussed alternatives with me, Lucas-babe. You just drop your decision on the table like a piece of muscle-tissue-meat-roast, and expect us to accept it. Perhaps you should have shared this problem with me before upsetting Raven. Husbands and wives do communicate, you know."

Because he was hurting, Lucas hit hard. "We sure did. Look where it got you."

"Maybe I'm happy here. Except for your stubborn streak, everything has been just lovely."

"You traded one bunch of needy relatives for another—" Lucas stopped, blinked and picked up his hat, which Chastity had neatly knocked off his head. "Why in the hell did you do that?"

"If you're going to feel sorry for yourself, you might as well do it without your hat. I've been wanting to do that for ages. Another thing..." She took a deep breath and propped her hands on her waist before continuing. Lucas had the feeling that she was winding up to hit him. He peered down at her cautiously. For a gentle, understanding woman, his wife could launch attacks that frightened him.

"Another thing that bothers me, since we're finally conversing, Lucas-babe, is that you have been holding back— emotionally and physically. I want you to talk to me, actually share your life—is that asking too much? And another thing, *I am not Alesha*. I will not break. I do not want to be treated like her." Chastity brushed her hands as though she had just tossed a dirty ball to him. "There. We're conversing. See how simple it is? I've laid out my problems. What are yours?"

"'Physically,'" Lucas repeated in a snarl. "You mean I'm not good in bed. Add that to losing my job and you—"

"You are too careful, Lucas-dear."

"You are pregnant, Chastity-sweetheart."

She lifted her chin, determined to challenge him. Despite his pride, Lucas admired the fine anger brewing within her. Chastity's cheeks turned pink, her green eyes glistening. "You've lost interest. You've taken your punishment, lived up to your honor by bringing me here and marrying me, and now *I'm not exciting to you.*"

A tear shimmered on the tips of her lashes and dripped to her cheek. "Honesty, that's all I ask. Admit you made a mistake and we can—"

"Don't say it." Lucas thought that she had never been more lovely, more feminine. Her lips trembled with emotions. "You're the most exciting woman I've ever known. You're so luscious and exciting I can hardly keep my hands off you."

Her expression lit up. "Really, Lucas?" All the tenderness was there, the sweet emotions tangling around his frayed nerves. "If you mean it, take me to the barn," she challenged softly. "But first tell Raven she's not losing her calf."

For days Lucas dealt with the echoes of Chastity's soft cries, the hunger on her lips and her body flowing into his. She loved him, gave herself fully to him, and he treasured each touch, each soft sigh, each scent. Fearing to love her fully, Lucas took what he could and gave it back twofold. He regretted that fear, damning Alesha for his scars.

The baby deserved parents who loved each other, and Lucas feared that he would fail again, unable to love Chastity. Fascinated by her warm, womanly instincts, he treasured her with his body and prayed that she would stay.

Two weeks later the well pump made odd grinding noises and he discovered that Chastity had watered her garden.

Chastity straightened from plucking a weed in her peas, slid her hand over the slight bulge in her abdomen. The baby had caused her to unsnap her cotton slacks waistband, and her tender breasts had enlarged. She scanned the Walkington land, smiled at the cattle and reveled in her happiness.

Lucas had begun taking time to talk to her. In fact, at every turn he told her exactly what bothered him.

The previous night he stared at her over a beautiful tossed salad and said flatly, "I like meat and potatoes. Salads don't cut it. A man's stomach can't be filled on fodder."

According to Lucas, the new fabric softener she had purchased with two detergent coupons smelled like flowers, and he wouldn't get caught in public wearing the scent. She learned that freshly ground pepper and coffee was for "people who have too much time." Hot tea was for sick people and elderly ladies. A new brand of soap bar caused an angry glare and a curse, something about being surrounded with women and flowers.

When she, Raven and Summer trimmed Wayne's curly coat to a proper poodle cut, Lucas held the dog on his hip. He plucked away the blue satin bow from Wayne's topknot and tossed it to the counter. Shooting them a menacing glare over his broad shoulder, he took Wayne with him to check the calves. "Don't ever sissify him again," he had ordered, holding the poodle like an endangered baby against him. He bent, sniffed Wayne's newly fluffed topknot and bit out, "Real dogs don't smell like perfume.

As he approached her now in the afternoon sunshine, Lucas's expression bore that same indignant look. He stopped at the end of her garden, tipped his hat back on his head with a jerk of his thumb and crossed his arms over his bare grease- and dirt-stained chest. "Having fun, lady? Watering your little garden to your heart's content?"

"Actually I watered this morning before the sun rose too high. The beans were looking droopy—" His scowl deepened and Chastity frowned. "What's wrong, Lucas?"

"Water gets tight out here. You're not in Chicago using a block hydrant. You've just washed clothes, taken a long shower and *you watered the hell out of the pump. The well is dry.*"

He jerked his thumb toward the patch of green grass in front of the house. "We've never had a grass yard before now. You know why, Miss Chicago Lady? Because of water. Of course there's one good thing, the faucets in the house will stop dripping."

Raven slid around the house to turn off the sprinkler and Summer's worried face peered out of the open kitchen window.

"According to the predictions, there's a drought coming. A bad one," Lucas continued, wiping his hand across his jaw and leaving a grimy streak.

"Lucas, you're in a dither. Calm down. Summer, bring your father a glass of iced tea," Chastity called.

"Save the tea," Lucas ordered tightly. "We'll need it to water the grass."

Raven touched Lucas's arm, her eyes brimming with tears. "Dad, I just took a bath and used a whole tub of water."

But Lucas was centered on Chastity, who began picking her way toward him over the beans and fresh green lettuce. "Lucas, you are much too excited," she began.

"Excited?" he repeated nastily. "Tell the cattle that this summer when they want water. We buy it in barrels and haul it in dry weather."

"You're selling Rosebud," Raven said quietly, tears streaking her pale face.

"No, he's not. There's plenty of water and I've just been offered two more part-time bookkeeping jobs. The girls want to help and they're re-designing fashions from Muggins's thrift store for resale. Remember that chambray dress Raven wore to church? She made it out of two of your old shirts.''

Lucas lifted his hat and ran his fingers through his hair with an air of deep frustration. "I don't know where you get the idea that there's water aplenty hereabouts. Whatever weird ideas you may have, *no Walkington female sleeping under my roof is going to take in work.*''

"Babe, I'm already working," Chastity sweetly reminded him.

"Then quit," he snapped, the muscle in his jaw working beneath the day's beard.

"Daddy!" Raven sobbed and ran toward the house.

Chastity angled her face up toward his. "I don't suppose you would like to retract that statement, would you, babe?"

He plopped the hat back on his head. "No."

"There is plenty of water here," she repeated quietly, despite the need to turn on the hose and cool Lucas from dusty hat to battered boots.

"Says who?" he shot back.

"The pregnant lady. I am a water witch, Lucas. There are three fingers of water beneath your land. Of course, you're so set on dishing out orders that *you're not listening to a word I say.*''

He stared down at her, clearly thinking the pregnancy had affected her mental processes. "Buttercup, maybe you'd better go lay down a bit. We can manage.... Maybe I flew off the handle—''

"The neighbors say that we're called dowsers in Oklahoma, but the principle is the same. Old Coot said I had his gift and I feel like there is water here, though I haven't had the time to research it properly." Chastity closed her eyes and wished for the control she possessed before Lucas entered her life. No one had ever stirred her into such a froth as her husband.

He lifted one eyebrow. "Are you serious? Have you told anyone else about..." Lucas cleared his throat "...about your gift?"

"Melody. She's promised to keep it a secret until you adjust to the idea. I thought I'd mention it again after you accepted the use of coupons and my other part-time jobs."

"You're quitting John's. Don't take on any more. All this has been too much for you." Lucas rubbed his hand against his jeans to clean it of dust and touched her hot cheek.

Now was no time to fall before Lucas's disarming tenderness. Chastity slashed his hand away and pushed her damp curls back from her cheeks. "No Walkington female who works can sleep under your roof, is that so?"

Forced into a corner, attacked by a woman who didn't like confrontations, but who had evidently been affected by her pregnancy, Lucas muttered, "Yep."

That night Lucas lay alone in bed, his hands behind his head because there was no sweet, soft, cuddling pregnant female to hold.

Chastity had installed herself in a tent in the shade of a maple tree. The large, airy tent was one he and the girls had used years ago. His wife's grim determination to work had unsettled him. Raven and Summer had helped her, lugged one of their mattresses into the tent and ran an electric cord from the house for a lamp.

Lucas answered the soft knock on his door and his daughters entered, wearing his discarded and patched cotton shirts for nightgowns. "Daddy? Were you sleeping?"

"Not rightly."

The twins moved to his window and looked at Chastity's tent. "Daddy, you've got to do something," Raven whispered.

"She's alone out there," Summer added unevenly.

"She'll cool down," Lucas said, though he feared that Chastity would pack and leave at any moment.

"You're so...so unromantic, Dad," Raven said, holding the curtain away from the window.

"Pregnant women are emotional," Lucas returned huskily. "She's a practical lady. She'll sort things out and come back inside."

"No," the twins answered at the same time. "We wouldn't."

The night had been long and in the morning, Chastity poured his morning coffee. The shadows under her eyes said she didn't sleep any better than he had. Lucas couldn't find the words to soothe her, and in the next two days, the house and the meals were weighted in tense gloom.

Hattie McCord's dented, dirty pickup soared down the dusty lane to his ranch. She drove right up to his tractor, surged her two-hundred-plus pounds out of the cab and stalked toward him. "So you're making that nice little wife of yours sleep out in a tent. What's wrong with you, Lucas Walkington? Don't you know a good thing when it's right under your nose?" she demanded, shaking her finger at him. "You ought to be ashamed. Getting that girl pregnant and not letting her be herself. She's a hardworking woman who wants to fit in. You keep tossing that Walkington temper at her and she's bound to head off for Chicago town. You'd better bend, Lucas. Before you lose that sweet little thing and that Walkington baby she's carrying."

Lucas stared at the dust cloud trailing after Hattie's pickup, jammed his hat on tighter and flooded the old tractor.

Ten

Lucas crossed his arms and leaned against the horse corral. He stared at Chastity's defiant little tent. The shadows of the trees danced around it in the moonlight, presenting a fortress that needed a siege. He knew better than to scoop up Chastity's soft body and plop her back in his bed. For a woman who professed to be calm and reasonable, his wife had issued a challenge no righteous Oklahoma rancher would turn down.

In the house, they skirted around each other warily and the twins found reasons to stay out of their path. Wayne deserted him for a soft, musical feminine voice and plates of special doggie goodies. Lucas considered the dog's desertion. He tried a low whistle that Wayne would recognize immediately.

The tent flap moved and a ball of white fluff hovered in the opening. He whistled again and Wayne barked sharply. The poodle ran outside, stood in the moonlight, then ran back into the tent. "A man's best friend," Lucas scoffed, jerking down the brim of his hat.

Damn. He'd always taken care of his family, working hard to provide for their needs.

The well had filled slowly, but to save water Lucas had taken their washing to the laundry near John's. Hattie caught him adding fabric softener and had raked him again about treating his family like some "foreign sheikh." She informed him loudly that women had rights and if working pleased them, then it was their God-given right to work.

While Chastity tended her garden and lived in her tent, Lucas chewed on being the laughingstock of Chip.

"Water witch." The word slapped the cool night air. "A Chicago water witch . . . a pregnant and barefoot one."

His cattle lowed in the moonlight and Lucas checked the starry sky for clouds. With luck a good thunderstorm would move through; then Chastity Beauchamp Walkington would have to head for the house. He pictured her in clinging wet clothing and groaned. Her swelling breasts and the tiny mound caused by his baby sensually stimulated him to a painful realization: Since they were married, Chastity and he had made love one or more times a day.

She said she loved him. Lucas had lost parents who loved him, and his daughters were growing away every day. He wanted that stubborn little tent-squatter to love him until eternity.

He kicked a rock across the corral. His wife made the world perfect when she wasn't holed up in that tent and her pride.

The next two days, the clear sky and a steady stream of visitors to Chastity's tent challenged Lucas.

The third night, Lucas ripped off his blankets, jerked on his jeans, plopped on his hat and walked out to his wife's new residence. The lamplight traced Chastity's silhouette on the canvas walls of the tent as she sat, working on her bookkeeping. Wayne barked excitedly, sliding through the flap and running toward him. Sidestepping the excited dog,

Lucas's bare heel hit a rock and he swore, hopping the remainder of the distance to the tent. He waited for Chastity to invite him into her canvas boudoir. When she didn't, he cleared his throat and waited.

After two minutes in which his temper started to rise, Lucas asked, "Chastity?"

"Who is it?"

Lucas inhaled, pressed his lips together and rubbed his injured heel against the mat that served as his wife's doorstep. "Lucas."

"Please come in." The formal invitation did nothing to soothe his wounded pride.

He pushed aside the flap, bent to enter the tent and stood inside it. Dressed in a light cotton nightgown with ruffles that touched her ankles, Chastity was beautiful. Freshly washed, her hair hung in long, natural sausage curls. Behind the round wire-rim glasses, her eyes filled with him, soft and mysterious. Moisture glistened on her lips and Lucas badly wanted to taste them.

To keep from reaching for her, Lucas jammed his hands in his pockets. The interior of the tent was as comfortable as his home, a small fan humming on a table that served as Chastity's desk. Several books and a lamp rested on another table near the neat bed. A bra strap escaped a pillow and Lucas suspected that Chastity hid it before he entered.

A pang of sweet pain shot through him—he missed the sight of her practical underwear.

Chastity poured him a glass of water from a covered pitcher and handed it to him as though she were entertaining company. That nettled his pride. "Please sit down, Lucas, you're..." Chastity glanced down his tall body, blushed and looked away. "You're so large, you fill the tent."

He stood there holding the glass of water and feeling like one-hundred-percent yahoo. "Where?"

Chastity sat on her bed, crossed her legs and adjusted her nightgown over them. "On my desk chair."

Lucas recognized it as one discarded and left in the barn. He eased into the wooden chair warily; it squeaked, protesting his weight. The night sounds of the crickets and tree frogs threaded the silence between them. Lucas cleared his throat and he glanced at Chastity, searching for a sign that she would yield. She stared back, smiled tightly and waited.

Lucas shot her a frown, eased his long legs out in front of him and took off his hat. "I hear you took on two new accounts."

She nodded solemnly. "Business is good."

"John Blue Sky says there's extra bookkeeping in the coupon business. Seems like folks around are doing more of it lately."

"Waste not, want not," she returned, tucking her bra strap beneath the pillowcase. The motion stunned Lucas; her breasts were warm and free beneath the light cotton. His hardening body reminded him that he had been days without Chastity's sweet love.

"Nice breeze tonight," he said, aching for the heat of her. Aching to be held and cuddled and knowing damn well he'd better skirt the issue of the extra bookkeeping jobs.

"Very nice." She lifted her arm to push back a jumble of curls and Lucas's body went taut. The pink rosebud spray across her breasts tightened, her nipples dark beneath the cloth.

"The well has filled back up."

"That's good." Chastity met his eyes, hers glittering and bright, reminding him of how he had jumped her for the dry well.

The thought that he had acted out of anger, hurting her, ripped at him. "Are you moving back in or do you like the Walkingtons being the gossip of the county?"

She sniffed, tilted her head defiantly and asked coolly, "So you haven't come to apologize, Mr. Walkington?"

"Not likely, Mrs. Walkington. I am concerned for you and for my baby. I want you to move back into the house. The problem with you is that you're used to taking care of other people. You're not letting other people—namely your husband—take care of you."

"*My* problem?" She inhaled sharply, spreading her fingers apart on the papers. "Your problem, Lucas Walkington, is that you do not trust anyone but yourself. I think it's time you change and share your life and responsibilities," she stated with an indignant little sniff.

"I've been sharing plenty. Come back to my bed," he returned warily, wanting to scoop her up and carry her into the night.

Chastity smoothed the gown over her crossed legs, and Lucas's throat went dry. "Clearly we are at an impasse."

"Reckon so."

Chastity's eyes slid away from his into the night beyond the flap. Her chin trembled and she hugged herself as though chilled. "Lucas, I think we both know the real problem. You made love to a Heartbeat Goddess and ended up with plain, practical me. Your pride won't let you admit that you've been cornered into marrying a woman you detest. A woman you have to force yourself to make love to—"

Lucas's roar shot out into the night. "What?"

She sniffed once, lifted her eyes, brilliant with tears, and continued in a husky, halting tone. "It's quite evident to me. You forgot yourself with Honey and ended up with me. I don't excite or satisfy you."

While Lucas thought how she excited and satisfied him until he couldn't think, her hands twined restlessly and she plucked at a ruffle swirling near her delicate arch. Lucas ached to stroke that arch, to kiss it and work his way upward— "I'm inexperienced, Lucas, but I want romance and love."

"Who the hell is going to romance and love you?" he demanded tightly, desperate with fear. If she left him for another man, he'd come apart.

Chastity adjusted her glasses primly. "I'm sorry that you don't find me desirable without my Honey disguise. Perhaps in the future there will be a man who—"

Lucas tried to cope with this development in his marriage, staring at her pale, averted face. He shook his head. "I don't find you desirable?"

"I'm just practical me, after all. I'm a woman who has always worked and I won't stop now. I won't be catered to, pampered and be kept outside my husband's heart because of another woman. You want Honey, pink sequins and all. I'm not willing to live with you while you love another woman. Except for Old Coot, I've never been a part of a family, not really... only when they needed me to get them out of scrapes. I grabbed the brass ring, greedy for you and a family to call my own, a family that I could love and cherish and share good and bad.... If you want to keep me outside your family, keeping the problems away from me that are a part of living and marriage, then I may as well stay here."

Stunned, Lucas stared at her, trying to form reason in his thoughts. "Damn," he said quietly after a long moment in which Chastity fiddled with her pencil. The pencil snapped in two as he continued to look at her. "I'm out of work, woman. That doesn't do much for a man's pride. You deserve more than what I can give you. That's a pawnshop ring you're wearing."

"Romance and love and a man's pride are all separate factors, Lucas. Since I can't help you in the romance and love mode, I've decided to help you as best I can. Maybe I can find a place in Chip, but I will not be a burden to you. I can support the baby and myself. Amazing things can happen with proper bookkeeping and filing."

Lucas thought about amazing things. Like her body fitting against his. He stared at her small foot, watched her toes and wondered if he'd ever sucked them one by one. Chastity inhaled, the motion drawing the light nightgown tightly against her breasts.

* * *

The image of the dark pink nubs pushing against the soft cloth remained with him long after he lay in his bed, staring into the moonlight. His wife wanted romance and love. Lucas flopped to his stomach and jammed his fists into the pillow. Chastity's warm, curved body nourished his baby and Lucas wanted her safe in his bed.

Lucas pushed his fingers through his hair. He'd played an honest game with Chastity, letting her know that he wanted her. While pregnant women had peculiar fancies, at four months Chastity wanted romance and love. Some women wanted pickles and ice cream, others craved midnight Chinese dinners. Chastity wanted romance and love.

He circled the thought. The soft pregnant little squatter living in that tent had slept throughout his maneuvering back to Oklahoma. He'd watched for cravings, prepared for them, and Chastity had blithely kept a healthy diet. He frowned, cuddling the pillow closer. Chastity had not shown signs of any unusual cravings…unless… Lucas slid his hand under the pillow to withdraw the practical cotton panties he'd just laundered.

They'd skipped a step from that "Heartbeats" weekend until they married. Every woman deserved her courting time filled with romance, flowers and sweet little nothings. Then there was dinner and dancing....

Short on money and facing a drought, he'd have to come up with unique proof that he loved Chastity. He wrapped his fist in the panties, an idea slowly taking shape as he pulled on a pair of jeans and went out to the porch.

For the next hour, he gripped the panties possessively and sat in the moonlight watching Chastity's tent. One thought kept returning: *Chastity had said she loved him.*

Wayne trotted down to the house, carrying a doggie chew bone. He dropped it at Lucas's bare feet. "She loves me, Wayne. It doesn't make sense, but she said she does."

The small warmth curling around his heart grew. A big neon arrow soared through his thoughts and pinged softly into his heart. Lucas said slowly, "Reckon I love her back.... Reckon I'm craving a little romance and love myself."

He grinned widely, tilting the chair back against the porch wall. Chastity Walkington wanted romancing and love and she was getting it. He would find a way to tell her that he loved what she was, who she was, not Honey on a "Heartbeats" weekend.

Within minutes, Lucas found himself standing in front of her tent. Banishing Wayne to the house with a pointing finger, Lucas eased inside the tent.

Chastity stirred in the shadows, nestling on the narrow bed. Both hands rested over her stomach and the child they had created. Lucas swiftly spread a quilt on the tent floor, stripped off his jeans and lowered his sleeping wife carefully to the pallet. She protested in a whimper, holding him tightly as he drew her to him.

Taking his time, Lucas nuzzled her throat, catching her sweet scent.

Chastity's fingers tightened on his shoulders, her nails gently, restlessly clawing. She sighed as he nibbled her mouth, tasting the sweetness clinging to the corners with his tongue. He smiled slightly as Chastity began moving over him, easing her knee across his thighs, sliding until she rested fully on top of him.

Closing his eyes, he stroked her back, cupped her bottom as she began rhythmically nudging her hips against his. A woman of action and purpose even in her sleep, Chastity ran her hand slowly down his body, nestling her face in the hollow of his shoulder. Lucas almost bolted when her hand curled around him, stroked and guided him inside her moist warmth. Afraid to move, fearing Chastity would awake and end the moment, Lucas shuddered slightly, holding back his pleasure as Chastity moved over him.

When he opened his eyes, dark green eyes stared down at him, her mouth curved in that mysterious half smile. "I won't break, babe," she whispered against his mouth.

Lucas lost himself in her sweet, hungry kiss, in the blending of her body with his.

He forgot why he couldn't open his heart to love.

With soft touches and heated kisses, Chastity pushed them over the edge, the flurry of heartbeats blending with the wind pushing against the tent. Her hand ran between them, touching him, then his cry of release met her soft sigh, the fever burning as they soared. At the last, his blood pounding violently. Lucas caught her near him. She lay by him in the aftermath, stroking his chest as the dawn sent streaking fingers against the night sky.

Unwilling for the dream to end, Lucas caught her to him desperately, his arms trembling as they enclosed her, fitting her spoon-fashion into his body as he drew a blanket over them.

Chastity snuggled into the cove of his thighs, turned slightly to brush a kiss across his lips and sighed sleepily. "Love," she whispered in a sigh almost covered by the sweeping wind.

Dozing in her warmth and fragrance, Lucas awoke in early morning. Chastity lay watching him, her chin braced on a hand resting over his heart. Her eyes came into focus slowly, a tendril of hair dancing with her breath. "Lucas, have you ever heard of double-coupon day?"

"No, but it sounds good," he returned huskily, aware that nothing separated them. Soft, warm flesh lay against him, her lips curving in a smile.

Taking his time, Lucas turned her beneath him, lowered his head to suckle her breasts and smiled against her scented skin when she arched against him. However angry Chastity was at him, she wasn't turning him away.

Her arches rubbed his calves, then stopped as he moved swiftly inside her, claiming her. Lucas kissed her hard, lifted his head and whispered, "You're mine, Chastity. Every ornery inch. We'll work out our problems and you'll have what you need...."

"Yes," she returned huskily, her body tightening immediately around him. "I'll have what I need."

She laughed later as Lucas stood at the tent opening and looked down at her curled in the bedding. One dainty arch raised to rub his jean-clad leg. "You'd better go."

Lucas cursed, scowled at the house and wondered why he bothered to shelter his daughters. Certainly they were old enough to know about romance and love. Distracted, wanting to stay wrapped in his wife's arms, he clasped the teasing little foot and bent to kiss her arch. Chastity gasped, her eyes darkening. "My, that was romantic, babe," she whispered in an awed tone.

His good mood didn't dim when Raven caught him crawling into his bedroom window—he'd been locked out of his bedroom. During the day he concentrated on his emotions, focusing on opening his heart and swapping his stiff-necked, old-fashioned pride for genuine acceptance of his wife's talents.

That evening Lucas slapped his saddle on Duke, tightened the cinch and began another moonlight ride. Sorting his life out in the midst of the girls' busy schedule and the various neighborly visits—which had increased since Chastity's little tent had appeared—wasn't easy. He listened to Raven, Summer and Chastity sing camp songs around a tiny fire, their voices settling around his lonely ache like a gentle balm.

He wanted his family all under the same roof. Wanted Chastity back in his bed. Impatience wouldn't solve their problems, it could threaten their marriage. He tugged at Duke's reins, seeking the shelters of the giant oak's shadows from the moonlight.

The country was dry, headed for drought— A series of feminine giggles drew his attention. Raven and Summer performed a cancan dance in the moonlight, Wayne leaping and barking around their legs. Directing the dance, Chastity stood in the moonlight, lifting her long cotton gown to lift a leg high. She pivoted, bent and motioned as if lifting the cancan skirts high.

Leaning his forearms on the saddle horn, Lucas watched her dance. A city woman dancing a cancan in a nightgown on an Oklahoma ranch was unique. The perfect candidate for his lifelong partner in romance and love.

Why hadn't he recognized that her pride equaled his own? Who was he to take her pride from her?

Chastity wanted to fit into his life, not remain protected and apart from his heartaches. If he wanted to keep her and his baby near, he'd better move fast.

Chastity watched Lucas pry a board from the old shed with a crowbar. The wood was seasoned oak, gray with weather and locked around its nails. Carl Murphy had arrived with his teenage sons at dawn, their pickup beds loaded with lumber. Immediately Raven and Summer had joined the work crew, dressed in their best jeans.

Their father, stripped to the waist and bronzed by the sun, was gorgeous. Chastity ran the flat of her hand across her stomach, calming the little twinges of happiness and the baby. For a woman who had never been stirred before her husband appeared, she found his nightly trips to her tent intensely romantic. Lucas always brought a small present—a bouquet of flowers from Hattie McCord's garden, a start of an herb, an antique canning jar for her collection or a discarded pioneer chest.

The past week they lay wrapped in each other's arms every night, exploring each other. Lucas told her about his parents, and the deep love of the land he had inherited. His boyhood was rich in love, his parents respecting and loving each other. He entered marriage with visions of the same happy life and found the dreams crumbled within weeks of the elegant wedding.

Then the twins, wanting a mother, had shopped throughout the county and had placed an ad in a singles column. Lucas had scampered around marriage-minded women for a year after the ad. Insecure at a young age, the twins needed Lucas's complete attention and he took them on special camping trips. When Raven was seven, she was certain she was adopted, though Summer was her exact image. They visited their mother and returned feeling gauche and ugly; Lucas's expression tightened when he relived Alesha's slap to Summer's cheek.

He taught them what he knew; how to change spark plugs or plow a field. He taught them the dances he had learned as a boy, to walk straight and proud. Then they moved into womanhood and Lucas floundered, the uncertain feminine temperament stunning him. He'd spoken too soon, or too sharply, frightened by the widening gap between himself and the twins.

Chastity had smothered her giggle against his bare shoulder when he told about lowering hemlines and ordering catalog dresses. She cried, learning of the young man saddled with guilt, working to keep the remainder of his inheritance and care for his children in the midnight hours.

She learned through Hattie of Lucas's deep pride in her adjustment to rural Oklahoma, in his daughters who were setting a fashion pace with refashioned clothing.

The weathered boards of the shed slowly became a pile as the men and the twins worked. When Chastity took iced tea to them, Lucas looked at the leaf of lemon balm herb in his glass and winked. "My wife's tea is the best in the county," he said quietly, his eyes warming on her. "She's starting an herb garden."

Chastity remembered when Lucas had placed aside his tea in her tent and had slowly kissed his way from her feet to her—she suddenly discovered that she was too hot, trembling as he bent to kiss her with icy moist lips. "Sweet," he whispered. "You're sweet all over."

After she shivered and wrapped her arms around her chest to hide her reaction, Chastity asked, "Why are you tearing down the shed?"

Summer and Raven took the empty glasses, grinning at her. "It's a surprise."

The next morning several neighbors arrived before dawn and Lucas pulled on his jeans with a curse. He bumped his head against the top of the tent and swore again. The tent threatened to topple and he gripped the center pole, steadying it. Chastity gathered her clothing desperately as the horns and the yells grew louder. When Lucas stepped outside the tent, wearing his jeans and a dark scowl, Hattie McCord shouted, "Honeymooners, get on down here. I'm starting coffee and breakfast. The whole county will be here at sunrise."

By late morning, the side porch was enclosed, the shed's weathered boards acting as paneling for "Chastity's business room." In quick slashes of conversation, Hattie informed her that siding and lumber were Lucas's as payment for his help with her cattle. "Hell," Hattie snorted. "You can even sleep in it if you want. Might save old Lucas from crawling through his bedroom window before the girls wake up. He can't figure out why the lock is sticking, but I'd say there are two girls who know why...they've been locking it every night from the inside and crawling out the window to come back in the house."

She winked and continued while Chastity blushed. "Found that out from Sam Fitzhugh, who came over to see if Lucas would help build fence. Sam saw Lucas crawl through the window and asked the girls about it. Old Lucas must be in love for sure to be sneaking flowers from my garden for you."

"Oh my," Chastity sighed, tears welling in her eyes. The next instant Lucas's arms were wrapped around her, his chin resting protectively on the top of her head. With trembling hands, Lucas smoothed her back, gathering her closer. "Buttercup, what's wrong?"

"I'm just so happy," she wailed, holding him to her with all her might.

After the immense potluck dinner, Lucas drew Chastity into the bedroom. He kissed her hungrily and picked her up in his arms, sitting on the edge of the bed. "I missed you, buttercup," he whispered in her ear. "Come back to me."

She leaned back, adjusting her steamed and tilted glasses to better see him. Stroking his jaw, loving him, Chastity whispered unevenly, "Oh, I miss you, too."

Nuzzling her neck and freeing tendrils from her braid, Lucas ran his hand slowly across her breasts and stomach. "How's the water witching business? I see you practice down by the elderberry bush."

She stiffened slightly, allowing his hand to rest over the baby. "Lucas, there is water there. I've followed Old Coot's instructions with a willow and a peach branch. Apparently my gift uses a peach branch, though the willow did tremble a little. Maybe I'm just not up to willows. Old Coot had a device that twirled, but I can't remember enough to make one."

"You're certain then?" he asked, nibbling on her ear.

"Positive."

"That's good because Harley Jones is on his way with well-digging equipment."

Chastity cradled Lucas's jaw with her hands and he kissed each palm, his expression tender. "What did you say, babe?"

"Harley Jones is a well-digger. You mark the spot and he'll dig," Lucas said, his palms cupping her breasts. "Are you nursing our baby?"

"Of course, but, Lucas, a well-digger... isn't that expensive?"

"Yep, reckon so. Can I watch you nurse the baby?" He lifted away her blouse, studying her breasts with the tip of his finger.

She flushed, uncertain of him and trying to balance well-diggers with Lucas's tenderness. "I...oh, Lucas, you realize that all the neighbors are outside, waiting for us... they'll want to see proof of my abilities—"

"Told them my wife was a gifted water witch. They're waiting for the show. Reckon they'll talk about it for years. Our son will be hearing about it in school—"

"Daughter," she corrected breathlessly, filling with happiness. "Oh, Lucas. You believe me."

Then he was kissing her with heart-stopping gentleness, cradling her and the baby. "More than believe, buttercup. Reckon I'm in love with you. Reckon it's time I told you so."

Her heart pounded, racing with emotions. She'd dreamed of his deep, sexy voice drawling those words someday. Her throat tightened, her fingers trembling as they stroked his warm cheeks. "Reckon?" she asked huskily, unevenly.

"Reckon I do, buttercup." One dimple enticed her exploring fingertips. "It's been a long time coming, hurt like sin paid back, but it was there, even when things were tangled. I knew inside that you were my heart, my dream, the day I met you."

The other dimple deepened. "Buttercup, I've been loving you without knowing it. Reckon I know it now."

"Oh, Lucas...." she whispered before his mouth closed over hers and he lowered her gently to the bed.

The exploring, sweet kiss promised a lifetime of tenderness and love; it whispered romance and excitement and curled around their hearts—

"Mr. and Mrs. Walkington," Hattie shouted beyond the locked bedroom door. "I got milking to do. If there's water-witching to be done, let's get at it." Lucas snorted, gathered Chastity tighter in his arms and lifted slightly to retort. Her finger pressed gently to his lips and he kissed it, distracted instantly. "You're certain, Lucas?" Chastity whispered, easing her fingers through his black hair.

"Love. One hundred percent, Mrs. Walkington." Then he grinned that dazzling high-voltage grin. "Buttercup, they're waiting for a water witch. It's been years since there was a dowser with a divining rod in the countryside."

"Oh, Lucas. What if I'm wrong? What if I've forgotten everything that Old Coot told me?"

"You believe in you, buttercup. I do."

"Oh, Lucas. Can we afford a well-digger? They must be expensive."

"Reckon Harley Jones is counting on a water witch. He thinks if you can find water, he'll be busy for a long time. It's an investment—he's got the idea that you're a working woman and might be interested in working part-time for him...when there's a need."

Her sea-green eyes widened for a minute, then her laughter curled warmly around him. "How I love you, Lucas-babe. You were worth every gold heart."

Chastity loosely held the forks of a vibrating, freshly cut peach branch. Old Coot had instructed her to concentrate, hold her breath and begin walking with her left foot.

The soil was dry beneath her feet, the grass tickling her arches. The silent populace of rural and Chip proper stood back from her. Looking tall and locked to his land, Lucas's hat shaded his face. She turned to him for a second, losing her concentration and winning a long, tender expression of love from her Oklahoma cowboy.

The wind rose suddenly, claiming her hair, sweeping the freed curls up and away from her face and caressing her skin. Chastity straightened her shoulders, ran her palm across Lucas's baby and closed her eyes, forcing her attention back to the stick in her hands. The peach branch jerked slightly just as the Old Coot said it would when water was near. She held each prong of the Y-shaped stick, allowing the end to lead her.

Lucas's heart pounded heavily against his chest. He'd forever remember Chastity poised in the sun and the dry June wind, her hair flying up and away from her face like a sunburst.

The wind pressed her clothing against his baby, a child made with desire and love.

There was learning and sharing to be done, long days and nights of opening his heart and telling Chastity of his love. Lucas inhaled the fresh air, realizing with pride that his actions—sweeping Chastity from Chicago to his ranch—were destiny. He had feared to love again, denied in his mind what his body defined for him.

The future waited, dressed in joy and love, sharing the hard times with Chastity and reveling in the good. Lucas glanced at Summer and Raven, at their intense young faces. With Chastity's help, he'd learn to bend, to understand his daughters' pride and needs.

Chastity allowed him to touch and explore her changing body. A gifted woman of tenderness and warmth, she had taken away his pain and given him love.

She followed the branch now, walking slowly toward the old elderberry bush. He walked a little ahead of the crowd, realizing that he would follow her path into eternity. The wind tugged at his hat and Lucas glanced at the clouds gathering in the horizon. Then Chastity stopped, the end of the stick bobbing toward the ground, and Harley's rig growled, moving closer to the spot.

Lucas moved quickly then, reaching his wife in four long steps and lifting her high into his arms, keeping her from harm. For once Chastity did not protest, curling her arms around him tightly as they watched. The boom on Harley's rig lowered slowly, the bit sinking into the ground.

After a few moments, Lucas settled in the shade of the old oak tree, holding Chastity on his lap. "It's deep, but a bigger vein than your well," she said finally, tiredly. "You'll need a pasture for the sprinklers."

"If we have the grass and the water, we can run more cattle...." Seeking to soothe her and ease his tension, Lucas rocked her in his arms and told her how he had bargained with Harley Jones. How Harley had refused at first, then reluctantly admitted that a success could bring business to his doorstep. Harley also had two left feet and needed help courting a reluctant schoolteacher who loved to dance. If ever Lucas felt like a yahoo, it was dancing in Harley's arms, issuing instructions and protecting his feet.

Hattie puffed up to them, carrying a small, rusty box. She handed it to Lucas. "This is yours, boy. It was just under an old root, wrapped in leather and old cloth. Got to get back," she said, returning to the crowd.

Lucas forced open the small box only to find another. Taking care, he snapped the rusty lock with his knife. The box opened and inside were small, carefully wrapped cloth bundles. The old gingham, rotted with time, fell away to reveal a woman's simple wedding ring. In another bundle ten large gold coins fell to the ground. "That's my great-grandmother's ring," Lucas whispered when he could talk. "Those ten coins were her dowry. My great-grandfather died years before she did . . . before she died, she was missing for a day . . . she must have come here, burying it. They say this was where he asked her to marry him . . ."

With trembling fingers, he lifted Chastity's finger and removed the pawnshop band to replace it with his great-grandmother's gold ring. "For my wife," he whispered unevenly.

"Love," he whispered slowly against the curling tendril brushing his face. The word was sweet and new to him, just like his wife. "Love," he repeated, and received a soft kiss.

Looking into his wife's teary willow-green eyes, Lucas barely heard the crowd cheer when Harley struck water.

Epilogue

Valentine's Day evening Lucas watched Chastity tuck Spring, their daughter, into her crib. His wife bent to kiss the baby good-night and Lucas enjoyed the soft rise of her backside beneath his long T-shirt.

Chastity's freshly washed hair, lightened by the sun and free from her daytime braids, now curled almost to her waist. The nursery's light outlined her curved body beneath the T-shirt. The clown lamp, earned with coupons, grinned knowingly at Lucas.

Standing by his daughter's crib, Lucas rested his hand on Chastity's waist and counted each day with her as a blessing. He kissed her temple, adjusted the glasses that had tilted, and shared the sweet moment with her.

Spring had arrived in the middle of November, delivered by Lucas. The midwife's car had stalled and at three o'clock in the morning they drove toward Muggins's hospital. He had pulled to the side of the road when Chastity had shuddered and said too quietly, "Lucas-babe, our baby is arriving—*now*."

Within half an hour, Spring arrived squalling hungrily. In another half hour, Chastity and the baby were in the hospital and Lucas had fainted into the bed next to his wife. Nurses hovered around him; Lucas could barely see his wife in the next bed. Easing to her side, he had bent to kiss her. "I love you, buttercup," he'd said, meaning it.

"I love you, too, babe," she whispered drowsily with that mysterious, intriguing, sloping smile.

"A sweet little girl—black hair," he remembered saying before he fainted again.

Now their daughter lay on her stomach, diapered bottom high in the air, and Lucas wiped away the tear that had been trailing down his cheek. With black curly hair and bearing the Walkington dimples, the baby added to their happiness. Love filled the house now, Summer and Raven laughing, preparing for college and meeting their challenges with his advice. They would enter college in the fall, and with Chastity's budgeting skills, they could continue.

He'd learned to open his heart, to share his fears and to bend his pride, though the task was often difficult. He'd learned that love worked both ways; love would build on trust and time.

Deep in his thoughts, Lucas straightened suddenly when Chastity's hand patted his backside, smoothing it. "Mother called today. She's learned how to balance her checkbook."

Within minutes, she turned the lock on the bedroom door. "Raven and Summer are staying with a girlfriend after the fashion show. That gives us the night, babe," she informed him as she removed her glasses.

The next instant, Chastity launched herself at him, her legs curling around his waist. The impact of her soft body caused him to brace one hand against the wall, the other cupping her soft, bare bottom.

"Oh, Lucas, I'm so happy. You were worth every gold heart."

Within minutes, Lucas lay tangled in her body, winded by the quick, hungry lovemaking they had just completed. He lowered his head to the pillow, kissed her damp throat. "Buttercup, we've got to work on our timing. I had a long, romantic Valentine's evening planned," he protested with a wide grin. "Every cowboy deserves a little romance."

She stirred beneath him, stroking his back. "We've got a lifetime to practice, babe. Tell me you love me again."

"Yes, ma'am, buttercup," Lucas whispered unevenly, obediently.

He whispered his love again during the night. Chastity hadn't lost the habit of inching over him in her sleep.

* * * * *

SILHOUETTE® Desire®

MYSTERY MATES!

Six sexy Bachelors explosively pair with six sultry Bachelorettes to find the Valentine's surprise of a lifetime.

Get to know the mysterious men who breeze into the lives of these unsuspecting women. Slowly uncover—as the heroines themselves must do—the missing pieces of the puzzle that add up to hot, *hot* heroes! You begin by knowing nothing about these enigmatic men, but soon you'll know *everything*....

Heat up your winter with:

#763 THE COWBOY by Cait London

#764 THE STRANGER by Ryanne Corey

#765 THE RESCUER by Peggy Moreland

#766 THE WANDERER by Beverly Barton

#767 THE COP by Karen Leabo

#768 THE BACHELOR by Raye Morgan

Mystery Mates—coming in February from Silhouette Desire. Because you never know who you'll meet....

SDMM

For all those readers who've been looking for something a little bit different, a little bit spooky, let Silhouette Books take you on a journey to the dark side of love with

SILHOUETTE Shadows™

If you like your romance mixed with a hint of danger, a taste of something eerie and wild, you'll love Shadows. This new line will send a shiver down your spine and make your heart beat faster. It's full of romance and more—and some of your favorite authors will be featured right from the start. Look for our four launch titles wherever books are sold, because you won't want to miss a single one.

THE LAST CAVALIER—Heather Graham Pozzessere
WHO IS DEBORAH?—Elise Title
STRANGER IN THE MIST—Lee Karr
SWAMP SECRETS—Carla Cassidy

After that, look for two books every month, and prepare to tremble with fear—and passion.

SILHOUETTE SHADOWS, coming your way in March.

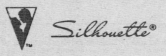
Silhouette®

SHAD1

Take 4 bestselling love stories FREE

Plus get a FREE surprise gift!

**Silhouette Books
is proud to present
our best authors,
their best books...
and the best in
your reading pleasure!**

Throughout 1993, look for exciting books
by these top names in contemporary
romance:

CATHERINE COULTER—
Aftershocks in February

FERN MICHAELS—
Whisper My Name in March

DIANA PALMER—
Heather's Song in March

ELIZABETH LOWELL—
Love Song for a Raven in April

SANDRA BROWN
(previously published under
the pseudonym Erin St. Claire)—
Led Astray in April

LINDA HOWARD—
All That Glitters in May

When it comes to passion,
we wrote the book.

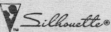 *Silhouette®*

BOBT1R